NIGHT
KITES

BOOKS BY M. E. KERR

Dinky Hocker Shoots Smack!

Best of the Best Books (YA) 1970–83 (ALA)
Best Children's Books of 1972, *School Library Journal*
ALA Notable Children's Books of 1972

If I Love You, Am I Trapped Forever?

Honor Book, *Book World* Children's Spring Book
Festival, 1973
Outstanding Children's Books of 1973, *The New York Times*

The Son of Someone Famous

(An Ursula Nordstrom Book)
Best Children's Books of 1974, *School Library Journal*
"Best of the Best" Children's Books, 1966–1978,
School Library Journal

Is That You, Miss Blue?

(An Ursula Nordstrom Book)
Outstanding Children's Books of 1975, *The New York Times*
ALA Notable Children's Books of 1975
Best Books for Young Adults, 1975 (ALA)

Love Is a Missing Person

(An Ursula Nordstrom Book)

I'll Love You When You're More Like Me

(An Ursula Nordstrom Book)
Best Children's Books of 1977, *School Library Journal*

Gentlehands

(An Ursula Nordstrom Book)
Best Books for Young Adults, 1978 (ALA)
ALA Notable Children's Books of 1978
Best Children's Books of 1978, *School Library Journal*
Winner, 1978 Christopher Award
Best Children's Books of 1978, *The New York Times*

Little Little

ALA Notable Children's Books of 1981
Best Books for Young Adults, 1981 (ALA)
Best Children's Books of 1981, *School Library Journal*
Winner, 1981 Golden Kite Award, Society of Children's
Book Writers

What I Really Think of You

(A Charlotte Zolotow Book)
Best Children's Books of 1982, *School Library Journal*

Me Me Me Me Me: Not a Novel

(A Charlotte Zolotow Book)
Best Books for Young Adults, 1983 (ALA)

Him *She Loves?*

(A Charlotte Zolotow Book)

I Stay Near You

(A Charlotte Zolotow Book)

Fell

(A Charlotte Zolotow Book)
Best Books for Young Adults, 1987 (ALA)

Fell Back

(A Charlotte Zolotow Book)
1990 Edgar Allan Poe Award
Best Young Adult Mystery Finalist

M. E. Kerr

NIGHT KITES

A Charlotte Zolotow Book
An Imprint of HarperCollins*Publishers*

Library of Congress Cataloging-in-Publication Data
Kerr, M. E.
    Night kites.

    "A Charlotte Zolotow book."
    Summary: Seventeen-year-old Erick's comfortable and
well-ordered life begins to fall apart when he is forced
to keep two secrets: the identity of his new girlfriend
and the nature of his brother's debilitating illness.
    1. Family problems—Fiction.   2. Brothers—Fiction.
3. AIDS (Disease)—Fiction   I. Title.
PZ7.K46825Ni 1986   [F]   85-45386
ISBN 0-06-023253-6
ISBN 0-06-023254-4 (lib. bdg.)

3 4 5 6 7 8 9 10

NIGHT
KITES

One

"I REALLY CARE about Nicki," Jack said. He paused to see if I was going to say anything. I wasn't.

He said, "She says I look like Sting."

"Well, you could be his son."

"I never think of rock stars having sons my age. They all seem about nineteen."

Jack was my age, seventeen. He was blond like Sting and green eyed like him, but he had a big nose Sting didn't have. He was self-conscious about it, so I liked Nicki for telling him that.

Nicki was blond and green eyed, too, and our age.

But Nicki was seventeen going on twenty-five.

The only really young thing about Nicki was her crushes on Sting and the other rock stars. Through most of high school her boyfriend had been Walter Ruski, known locally as Ski. He wasn't in school. He was older. He was the closest thing to a Hell's Angel we had around Seaville, New York. He was a scuzzy character but good-looking. Very. He was the type who wore punk bondage stuff and got around on a Kawasaki. He wore a lot of crosses around his neck, a Reaper of Death ring, and black hair, and was always in black, with black motorcycle boots and anklets with spike clips. . . . I could see a girl falling for Ski. He was a dark hero. You see them all over rock videos.

Jack and I were having this conversation on a day in early September, out in the bleachers of the Seaville High stadium.

Down on the field they were trying out new pom-pom girls. My girl, Dill, was one from last year, but Nicki was a hopeful.

I didn't think Nicki'd make it. It wasn't even her idea to try out—it was Jack's. If I'd been Jack, I wouldn't have talked her into it. Not that Nicki couldn't jump as high as the other girls, or shout as loud, and she had the looks, too. She really had the looks. . . . But I knew how the other girls felt about Nicki Marr. There was no way, I didn't think, they were going to let her be one of them.

"Do you like her, Erick?" Jack finally asked me. "She thinks you don't like her."

"Tell her I like her fine."

"I hope you mean it."

"I do," I told him. What could I say? It was already too late.

"She hasn't had it easy," Jack said.

I didn't know her whole story. I knew her mother'd died a few years ago. Her mother'd run a small women's clothing shop called Annabel's Resale, which was attached to Kingdom By The Sea on the dunes outside of Seaville. At one time Kingdom By The Sea had been a big summer tourist attraction. It was a motel that looked like a castle, with towers, domed roofs, even a drawbridge. Her dad owned it; everyone called him Captain, because there was sort of a nautical air to the place. But in recent years it was judged to be an eyesore. The more money that poured into Seaville, the more people didn't want that kind of circus sitting right on the outskirts of the village. So there were all sorts of petitions circulating against it, business was falling off, the paint was starting to peel: It looked like an old, run-down amusement park. . . . Nicki lived out in that place.

Jack was my best friend all through grade school, middle school, and high school. We lived on the same street. We liked the same things. We wore the same clothes, both of us sitting there that afternoon in our 501 jeans, our muscle shirts, our Nikes. We were from the same mold, it looked like.

There were plenty of differences, physical and family. I was redheaded like all Rudd males. (I looked enough like my older brother, Pete, to be his twin,

even though there was a ten-year age difference.) I
was never the star athlete Jack was. I wasn't heavy
enough for football, like Jack, or tall enough like Jack
for basketball. Tennis was my game, golf, sailing. Jack
could do all those things well too, though the Case
family wasn't in The Hadefield Club and Jack didn't
own a boat. (He didn't need one as long as I owned
one; anything of mine was his.)

Jack's dad lived and worked in Seaview as an elec-
trician. Mine was a corporate Wall Street man, with
an apartment in New York City. Mine came out to our
house only on weekends, usually.

But until Nicki came into Jack's life, any differences
between us didn't make any difference: We were two
peas in a pod. Even though Jack never had a steady
girl and I dated only Dill, our double dates were easy.
We never had to think about how the girls would get
along together. They just did.

I'd spent most of the past summer in New York City,
working as a runner for Rudd & Lundgren, my father's
investment firm. When I came back to Seaville to start
senior year, Dill told me that Jack was seeing Nicki.
It was big news to Dill, too. She'd been working in
the Catskills as a waitress, to earn money for college.

I said, "Nicki will mop up the floor with poor Jack."

"We both know why he's dating her, right?" Dill
said.

After Ski, there'd been Bucky Moon, then T. X. Hoyle, both pretty smarmy characters, sort of charming smarmy, the kind with a little flair, but the kind who ran on the fast track, and you gave a lot of room to on the sidewalks.

One night right after Labor Day Jack asked us to join Nicki and him. They were going to see a Stephen King movie; they were going out to Dunn's Drive-In after.

Nicki had her own technique for handling social situations. She ignored Dill totally. Dill was directing conversations at her, and saying her name at the beginning and end of every sentence, to make her feel included. She was complimenting her on her clothes. Nicki always came away from tacky old Kingdom By The Sea looking like a fashion ad. Dill said it was because she wore all the designer clothes from Annabel's Resale, which Nicki's aunt had been running since her mother died.

Nicki looked right past Dill to me. Nicki spent the evening featuring Jack and me. She flirted with both of us, as though we were both her dates. It was easy to see why Nicki didn't have any girl friends at Seaville High. Nicki didn't relate to other females.

She was the type who could make a seductive number out of passing you a plastic fork. Her fingers found yours at the same time her eyes did, and both of them caressed you. It was that sort of thing all night.

As we were getting ready to leave Dunn's, we all started to pile into Jack's old Mustang. Dill'd already crawled into the back. I had to ride up front with Jack; I was going to jump out to buy dog food on the way home.

"See, I never ride in back when I can ride up front," Nicki said.

She rode up front between Jack and me.

Her leg pressed against mine, even though there was plenty of room. Every time she said something, she touched my knee with her hand.

She talked about Sting.

She said, "Jack looks like him, doesn't he, Erick?" Hand on my arm that time, lingering there. She said, "Jack, do you think you could write a song like 'Every Breath You Take' or 'Every Little Thing She Does Is Magic'?"

I felt the pressure of her fingers. I smelled her perfume.

Jack just laughed.

That September afternoon when the pom-pom girls finished their routines, Nicki and Dill came into the bleachers to get us. They didn't walk up the steps together. Nicki was in front, and Dill was trailing behind her.

I loved Dill's looks. She had a style that was both sweet and tough. She was pretty, but she was also boyish. She had this great face: strong white teeth, always a tan left over from summer, straight black hair she liked to wear very short, slicked back almost like a boy's cut. That day she had on the gold hoop earrings I'd given her for her birthday. She didn't have Nicki's full figure—she had practically no breasts. She had a shy way of talking out of one side of her mouth, as though what she was saying had to be sneaked into any conversation. But Dill wasn't really shy. She was more innocent than shy. I was her first real boyfriend.

"Look at her!" Jack said about Nicki. "Just look at her!"

I looked. Looking at Nicki was what you did. You *looked*.

I don't think I'd ever seen Nicki in pants, not even when she was on the back of Ski's motorcycle. She just never wore them. Dill was in a skirt that day too, the pom-pom outfit, with the very short maroon skirt and the white sweater.

But Dill usually wore Guess? jeans or cords. Nicki wore outfits, costumes: that day some kind of navy-blue knee-length sweat shirt with yellow Day-Glo socks and dark gladiator sandals. You didn't expect such a thin girl to fill out a baggy sweat shirt the way Nicki did. You expected the long, thin legs, and she had very long, blond hair, the soft, shiny kind that fell over one eye.

Nicki was always brushing it back to look at you with these light-green eyes, as though she was sizing you up, as though she was telling you she could handle you no matter who you were. It seemed to me one eyebrow was always raised a little, like she was questioning you silently about something. Don't ask what.

Maybe Jack was reading my mind, because he said, "It isn't just the way she looks, either."

"Well," I said. I didn't know what to say. The idea of my old buddy being that gone on someone was totally new to me. Neither Jack nor I were big makeout artists—neither of us had ever made out 100%. But Jack was the one who always had to be talked into dates. Dad called Jack The Neanderthal Man. There was something clumsy and jock about Jack. He'd never even learned to dance.

Then Nicki was standing there smiling at us, holding Jack's arm with one hand, playing with his fingers with her other hand.

"How'd it go?" Jack said. "Are you a pom-pom girl?"

"I don't know yet," Nicki said. "I don't really care."

I thought, That's all Dill needs to hear. Dill was one of these gung-ho high school girls who'd have run away from home if she hadn't made pom-poms.

"We vote tonight," Dill said.

Nicki looked directly at me. "Would *you* vote for me, Erick? Tonight?"

Yeah, I'd have voted for her. Maybe not for pom-pom girl.

We were all laughing but Dill.

Two

ONE TIME my brother, Pete, made me a night kite. Pete said sure, most kites fly in the daytime, but some go up in the dark. He made the kite himself. He put little battery lights on it, and we sat on the sand down in front of The Hadefield Club, watching this diamond-shaped thing blink out over the ocean, its phosphorescent tail glowing under the stars.

There was the sound of ocean waves and the salt smell in the damp air. I was five and Pete was fifteen.

I said the kite might get scared in the dark. Pete said night kites are different, they don't think about the dark. They go up alone, on their own, Pete said, and they're not afraid to be different. Some people are different, too, Pete said.

I said, "Pete? I don't get any of Dad's jokes."

We'd left our folks back up in the dining room of The Hadefield Club, eating dinner with Grandmother and Grandfather Rudd. They were visiting from Pennsylvania, and Grandfather Rudd was doing his usual number, complaining about the food and the way people in the dining room were dressed ("There are men here without ties on—I'm surprised"), and finding fault with anything Dad said about his work, too. . . . Dad did what he always did when this happened: He started telling jokes.

Pete and I had polished off our club steaks while they were still going at their lobsters. Dad was telling one joke after the other. Pete was guffawing in that loud way that was phony. I was squirming in my chair, gulping down ginger ales, and showing Pete how to fold his napkin to make rabbit ears.

"You said you had something to show Erick when it got dark," Dad said to Pete. "It's dark."

We excused ourselves, got the kite from the car, and walked down to the beach."

"What joke didn't you get?" Pete asked me. "You got the one about the guy who bought stock in an umbrella company, and a few months later it folded?"

"I got that one. I didn't get the one about the arbor, arbor—"

"The arbitrage trader who believed in reincarnation, and wanted to come back as a perpetual warranty," Pete said. "It's too complicated to explain, and it's not that funny. What's important is to know why Dad tells those jokes."

"Why does he?"

"Because he's nervous. Because Dad doesn't know how to deal with Grandpa. Dad should say to Grandpa, 'I brought you here because I thought you'd enjoy it, and I'm sorry if you don't,' and he should tell Grandpa to just butt out of his business dealings. Grandpa doesn't know anything about investment banking. But Grandpa gets to Dad, so Dad tells jokes. He doesn't know how to talk."

"He talks to us."

"Even with us he mostly gives advice, or orders. Be in by eleven, wear a tie, cut your hair, did you take out the trash, do your homework? That's not really talking, Ricky. Mom talks, but Dad doesn't know how."

"Do I know how?"

"We're talking right now. We're talking about being scared, and people who are different, and we're talking about not being scared to be different. . . . Look at that kite dance up there! I think it likes the dark!"

I wasn't so sure. There was something slightly eerie about that night kite. But I was always the cautious, conservative type—the last one in the water.

Pete had been a fan of *Star Trek* when he was younger. He'd chased off to all the Trekkie conventions in New York City. His favorite character on the show was Mr. Spock, the Vulcan with the pointed ears and no emotions, played by Leonard Nimoy.

Pete knew every episode. His favorite was one called

"Counter-Clock Incident." It was about a reverse uni-
verse, with black stars shining in a white space, and
people who were born old and died young.

Pete got me to watch a rerun of that with him once,
around the same time he made that night kite. It terrified me to watch the *Enterprise* crew turn into children, losing their knowledge and their space skills.
Pete couldn't believe I was actually afraid, but there
was the big difference between us—Pete was the dare-
devil, the adventurer. My favorite character on that
show was everyone's hero, Captain Kirk. I never liked
anything too exotic or oddball.

Even though I tried to be more like Pete, I always
came off more like Dad. I sensed how badly Dad always wanted to fit in. He'd married into money, old
money, not the glitzy new kind. Mom's family practically founded Seaville. Dad had spent years trying
to prove he was good enough to be one of them . . . plus
all his life trying to get Grandpa Rudd to think he was
anything but a loser. I felt for Dad, even when I was
little, and I told Pete that night on the beach, "Dad
thinks people don't like him."

I could see Pete's freckles in the moonlight, and his
mouth with that little half smile. "You know that about
Dad, hmmm? Good boy!" Pete said.

"That's why Dad always says our family is first, maybe.
Family will always like you."

Pete chuckled and mussed up my hair. Dad was

always saying our family was first. I liked hearing it.
I knew too many kids whose folks split up. I liked the
feeling nothing like that would ever happen to us. "You
boys sow a lot of wild oats *before* you marry," Dad'd
tell us, "because Rudds marry forever!"

We kicked around the idea of Dad not knowing how
to talk, and some other ideas: Mom was the one to
approach if you didn't want to go in the direction Dad
was pointing you toward. Dad was the one with good
common sense—go to him for practical advice. Count
on Mom's heart. Count on Dad's head.

We wound up as usual with Pete telling me to make
up my own mind about people, though.

"Don't ever let me influence you. Don't let anyone
tell you how to think. . . . But try not to be too tough
on people."

I said, "Life is hard and then you die." Pete had a
T-shirt with that written on it.

"Yeah," Pete said.

"Would you rather be a night kite or a day kite?" I
asked him.

"Oh, I'm a night kite."

I figured myself for the regular day kind.

I figured Nicki Marr was probably a night kite. She
not only didn't seem to mind being different from the
other girls, she seemed to go for it.

Tuesdays and Thursdays I worked at The Seaview

Bookstore, from five in the afternoon until nine at night. The store was right in the village, on the main street near the movies, so we got a lot of customers on their way to and from Cinemas I, II, and III.

The day of the pom-pom tryouts was a Tuesday, and I'd gone from there to work. When I came out of the bookstore that night, Nicki was standing there. The night, like the day, was unusually warm, more like summer than fall. A lot of people were strolling around. We always did good business on nights like that.

"I came by to pick you up," Nicki said. "I'm staying in the village at my aunt's tonight. Daddy's got the whole V.F.W. out at Kingdom, so he wants me out of the way."

Nicki was always dressed in a way Dill would dress for special occasions. She had on a black oversized camp shirt over a white tank top and a black-and-white-striped skirt. She was one of those girls who smoked on the street, something my mother always complained was too tacky for words.

"Jack's home studying for the French test tomorrow," she said. "I should be studying, too, but I'm flawed. I just talked to Dill, and she's studying, of course. You don't have to, though, do you? You're something of a star in French class." She smiled at me. I was still trying to get used to the idea she'd come by the store for me.

Then she took my arm and said why didn't we walk

around for a while? Nobody ever took my arm, except my mother sometimes in St. Luke's Church, on our way up or down the aisle, and I was always awkward crooking my elbow, walking that way. Dill and I usually held hands. There was something almost formal about going around with someone's arm in yours.

Nicki was right at ease. We started up the street, past the movies and Paper Palace.

"How come you talked to Dill?" I asked her.

"She called to tell me I didn't make pom-pom girl."

I was trying to think of something sympathetic to say when Nicki laughed. "I thought we'd celebrate. You can buy me a Coke at Sweet Mouth."

I said okay. I said, "Why did you try out for pompom if you really didn't want it?"

"You know why. Jack wanted me to. Jack wants me to be one of them. He's one of them, so I suppose I should try to be one of them."

I was thinking that I was one of them, too. Didn't she know that? Jack and Dill and I were part of that whole Seaville High scene, part of *the* crowd.

"Does Jack know you planned to pick me up?" I asked.

"Did I plan to pick you up?" She bumped against me lightly, purposely, and laughed, as though there was a double meaning to the "pick me up" part of the sentence.

I felt a little sorry for her. I remembered Pete telling me Dad told jokes when he was nervous. Maybe Nicki flirted when she was.

When we got to Sweet Mouth, I held the door open for her. It was crowded. It was the kind of night that brought kids into the village to hang out. Every head in the place turned when we came through the door, then turned again for a second look.

I knew most of the kids there. I said hello, hi, how ya doin', all the way across the floor, to the table for two. Nicki didn't greet anyone. She didn't let go of my arm until we got to the table.

Roman Knight was there. He was the senior class wiseacre, a glitzy character, easily the richest kid in school, and the smartest, too. His dad was an international talent agent. He was the kind of kid who spent summers at the family villa in the south of France.

"Hel-*lo, Nicki!*" he called out, but he wasn't really talking to Nicki. He was showing off for everyone's benefit, making some other cracks to the group with him. I knew the kind of cracks. She seemed to invite them. When she was hanging around with Ski, she even seemed to enjoy them, tossing her long hair back, hanging on to Ski on his Kawasaki, giving everyone the finger behind her back.

"Roman Knight is a sleazeball," she said as we sat

down. She fished a Bic lighter out of her pocket and put it down on the table. Then she put a Merit 100 in her mouth.

I took the hint and lighted her cigarette.

She was a no-hands smoker.

"Do you know how Roman got his name?" I asked her.

"I don't care how a scumbag gets his name," she said.

I told her anyway, grateful for any subject of conversation. I was getting that trapped feeling: What the hell was I going to talk to *her* about?

"Roman was supposed to have been conceived on a night in Rome, after lots of champagne," I said.

"See, I don't care about Roman Knight or any of that crowd," she said. I don't know what crowd she thought I was in.

We ordered Cokes.

"Jack's birthday is the first weekend in October," she said. "Bruce Springsteen's going to be in New York that weekend. I thought we could all go."

"Jack doesn't know Bruce Springsteen from Rick Springfield," I said.

"He says he likes him."

"He's just saying that to please you."

"Well, he's right. That pleases me. . . . Jack says your dad has an apartment in New York he never uses on weekends."

"Do you know how hard it is to get tickets to a Springsteen concert?" I said.

"We could watch everyone go in, if we couldn't get tickets. Then we could see New York."

"It costs an arm and a leg to see New York, Nicki."

"Just *see* it. See Times Square. See Greenwich Village."

"See us all get mugged," I said.

"Jack says he'd love to get away for a New York weekend."

"If that's what he said, okay, I'll ask my father—but don't count on seeing Bruce Springsteen."

"I never *count* on anything," she said.

When our Cokes came, she put out her cigarette, picked up a fresh one, and waited for me to give her a light.

"Don't say anything to Jack until you've asked your dad, okay?" she said.

"I can ask him tomorrow night. He's coming out to dinner with my brother."

Nicki said she didn't even know I had a brother. Where was he?

"He lives in New York. He's ten years older than I am."

"What does he do?"

"He teaches French and English at a private school, but he really wants to be a writer. He writes science fiction."

I told her about the one story Pete had published. It had won all sorts of prizes. It appeared in a little magazine called *Fantasy*. It was about a world where everyone was both male and female except these characters called Skids. They were male or female, not both, and they needed each other to reproduce. . . . Pete's story, called "On the Skids," was about a male and a female who fell in love, and were being hunted down for "skidding," which was against the law.

Since Pete had written it, it'd appeared in a lot of anthologies. Pete was expanding it into a book. He would work on it off and on. He was always upstairs typing away on something when he still lived with us.

I told Nicki about Pete's world, called Farfire, and the inhabitants, called Farflicks, who were all capable of self-fertilization. I told her that I'd been the first one in the family he'd tried it out on, and how Dad said Pete'd been dining out on that little short story for all of his adult life.

Nicki Marr wouldn't win any Best Listener prizes. Some people listened to other people's conversations while you were talking to them; Nicki listened to songs. Her eyes were glazed over while I talked, and Bryan Adams sang "Somebody" in the background. She tapped her fingers on the side of her Coke glass and seemed to be whispering some of the words to herself, the cigarette dangling from her lips.

She finally said, "Bryan Adams used to wash dishes in a restaurant."

Then she said, "I'm sorry. You were talking about your brother."

"Pete."

"That's why you're so good at French? He teaches it?"

"Pete and I talked French when we were little," I said.

Mom had grown up bilingual. She was speaking French by the time she entered kindergarten. She used to talk with Pete in French most of the time. Dad finally stopped her doing it with me. Dad was rotten at languages. He didn't like being left out that way.

Nicki said, "I still remember that French poem you translated for class two years ago. I've never forgotten it. Are you surprised?"

" 'Poem to the Mysterious Woman,' " I said.

"Yes."

Pete got the credit for that one. He loved that poem. Old Stamiere, who'd been teaching French at Seaville High since the building was erected, remembered that, and made some crack after class about next time finding a poem on my own—"You're Erick Rudd, aren't you? Not Peter Rudd."

Nicki was playing with some keys. She had long,

thin fingers, and long nails, manicured but not colored. They were the kind of hands you imagined did nothing but arrange flowers in vases or stroke Persian cats, or touch silk and velvet. Dill had little square hands that felt small in mine, the way my hands, when I was little, must have felt in Pete's.

"Say something from that poem, can you?" Nicki asked me.

" *'J'ai tant rêvé de toi que tu perds ta réalité.'* "

"Now in English."

"*You* take French," I said.

"Something about dreaming of someone too much."

" 'I have dreamed of you so much that you lose reality.' "

She didn't say anything right away. There was some song of Madonna's playing. I was thinking that she looked a little like Madonna. She was looking out the window, where there were some kids on bikes under the streetlight, talking. Beyond them, people were sitting on the benches outside the A&P, enjoying the warm night.

"It reminds me of something my mother'd write," Nicki said when she looked back across the table at me. "My mother did this automatic writing? She was sort of psychic. She'd go into her room and just write these poems she said came to her from the spirit world. They were all love poems."

"In French?"

"Not in French, no. They were in English. . . .
After she died, you read that poem in French class.
And you know what I thought?"

"What'd you think?"

"I don't think it anymore. Right after someone dies
you'll think almost anything."

"What'd you think?"

"I thought she was coming back through you."

She picked up her keys and ground out the cigarette
in the ashtray. "My mother was a little bent, but in a
nice way. She believed Siamese cats carry messages
from the beyond. Do you like Siamese cats?"

"I don't know any," I said.

"I'll introduce you to some," she said. "We've got
six of them out at Kingdom."

She was pushing her chair back, ready to go.

I wouldn't have minded staying.

Three

"WHERE'S THE BOTTLE of wine I brought out for dinner?" Pete asked when we were all seated under the crystal chandelier in the dining room. He had on a sweater and cords, like me. His looked really baggy on him, he was so skinny. He said he'd picked up some kind of amebic dysentery in France last summer.

If there was anything going around, it always found its way to Pete. If he didn't have something wrong with him when he came out to Seaville to visit, he came down with it immediately. Something between Dad and Pete brought out every kind of symptom from hives to postnasal drip.

"I put the bottle in the wine cellar," said Dad.

As usual, Dad was in a business suit and tie. Dad had the Rudd red hair, but he was losing it now and, like Mom, putting on a little weight. But Mom was the dramatic type (directing *Come Back Little Sheba*

for the Seaville Players that fall), and she hid her weight
under capes and caftans. She had on a long white caftan
that night. Her ash-blond hair was held back with a
white ribbon; her blue eyes were shining, as they
always did when Pete was home.

Pete said, "That's a good cabernet. I picked it out
very carefully for this occasion."

"You and your mother already had two martinis,"
Dad said. "Since when do you drink so much?"

"Arthur. Darling. It's a special occasion. Pete's home."

"So am I," Dad said. "I don't like to see my son
turning into a lush."

"You're home every weekend," Mom said.

Pete got up while Mrs. Tompkins was putting down
the soup bowls. "I'll get it."

"Your soup will get cold," Dad said.

"I'm going to skip the soup."

"It's cream of broccoli your mother made especially
for you."

"He can skip the soup if he wants to," Mom said.
"But you're so thin, Pete."

I kept my mouth shut. You never knew when things
were going to explode between Pete and Dad. Mom
once said their problem was they both wanted to be
autonomous. That's when I learned the word autonomous, which means subject to its own laws only. I
pulled it on Dill once, when we were having the usual

argument in the backseat of Jack's Mustang.

I said what kind of a relationship was it, anyway, when she wanted to be autonomous? Dill said I don't know where you got that word, but it's going to take more than a big word to change my mind on this subject. What's it going to take? I said. . . . A big gold wedding band, she said, sometime in the future, after I've worn the small diamond engagement ring for a while.

When Pete left the dining room, Dad pulled his chair back, lifted the tablecloth, and said, "OUT!"

Oscar, our fourteen-year-old English bulldog, crawled out from under the table with his head down and wobbled into the living room. He was really Pete's pet; Pete had gotten him for his thirteenth birthday.

"I know we do a lot of things around here in honor of Pete's infrequent visits," Dad said, "but dining with a dog that smells like a dung heap under the table isn't one of them."

"Poor old Oscar," Mom crooned.

Mrs. Tompkins was headed back into the kitchen when the phone rang. Dad told her to tell whoever it was calling that we were having dinner.

Pete poked his head through the door. "Erick? It's Dill. She's calling from a pay phone."

I said I wouldn't be long and Dad scowled.

While I walked toward the kitchen, I heard Mom

say, "Don't be cross, darling. Please. Not tonight."

Pete was opening the wine. Mrs. Tompkins was taking a rib roast out of the oven. She was a big, blond widow who'd worked for us since before I was born and had an apartment over our garage.

"Erick?" Nicki said. "I just said it was Dill."

"What's up? We're eating."

"I just wanted to tell you the first weekend in October is perfect. There's no game that weekend. It's the one weekend Jack doesn't have to play."

"I doubt that we can get tickets, Nicki."

"Tickets to what?" Pete whispered.

"Bruce Springsteen," I said. "Don't get your hopes up, Nicki."

"But we could go in anyway. Couldn't we?"

"I'll ask Dad," I said. "Are you sure Jack wants to?"

"I already hinted around, and he does."

When Pete and I got back into the dining room, Dad said, "Who's the fourth glass for?"

"There're four of us, aren't there?" Pete said.

"Your brother doesn't drink."

"He may have one glass," Mom said, "if he promises to paint the kitchen chairs."

"Sneaky," I said. She'd been after me to do those chairs.

"Do all the teachers at Southworth School drink?" Dad asked Pete.

"Yes, sir," said Pete. "I think it's because they all regret not choosing business careers where they can make upward of sixty and seventy thousand a year."

"Oh, Pete." Mom giggled. "Pete."

"Yes, encourage his sense of humor," Dad said sourly. "He needs it when he cashes his paycheck."

"Pete," Mom said, "tell him."

Pete got to his feet.

"Tell me what?" Dad said.

"Hold your horses," Pete said. "I want to make a formal toast."

"A toast!" Mom said. She held up her glass. I held mine up, too. Dad looked reluctant, but he went along with it.

"Here's to all of you for *not* asking me how my novel was coming along, more than once or twice a year."

"We were afraid to ask," Dad said.

"Wait!" Mom said.

"For your faith in *The Skids*. Particularly *you*, Mom."

"Did you sell it?" Dad asked.

"There's a Hollywood producer who's interested in it for a screenplay, or a TV series. Shall we drink to that?"

We all clinked our glasses together.

"Congratulations, Pete!" I said.

"Isn't that good news?" Mom said.

"I didn't know you'd finished it," Dad said.

"It's not finished. I have five chapters and an out-
line."

"Oh, it's not even finished?" Dad said.

"I don't have to finish it. I'm going to turn it into a
screenplay."

"It'll make a superb movie!" Mom said. "Or TV
series!"

"Well, that's good, Pete, that's good," Dad said.

"Pete might make enough money to leave Southworth," Mom said.

"I don't know about that," Dad said.

Somehow during the middle of dinner, after Pete
finished filling us in on all the details about this producer, who thought *The Skids* was a hot property, the
subject of S.A.T. scores came up. I know I didn't bring
it up. I was going to take the S.A.T. over again in
October. I'd gotten a 500v and a 580m. Pete had gotten
a 700v and a 720m when he'd taken them. But typi-
cally, Dad wasn't on my back about my scores; he was
on Pete's back about Pete getting such good grades all
through high school and college, then "throwing
everything out the window" to be a prep school
teacher—"Not even," Dad threw in, "a university professor—I could live with *that*."

"I offered to stay at Princeton and finish my Ph.D.,"
said Pete.

"You *offered*?" Dad sputtered. "Who needs such an

offer? That's an offer I find easy to refuse! Education is a privilege, not something you *offer* to put yourself through to please someone else!'"

"Well, now we don't have to worry about it," Mom said. "Pete's going to get to work on this screenplay."

"Fine," Dad said to Pete, "but don't leave Southworth."

"Don't leave Southworth? You're always telling me it's a dead end!"

"It is, but at least it's a bird in the hand."

"So is this. I might make enough to write full-time."

"You'd be better off using the money to go back to graduate school," Dad said. "You could teach at a university and write on the side. Philip Roth does that. Many writers do."

"I can't afford to go back to graduate school *and* support myself writing!"

"You can't afford *not* to, Pete!"

It was the same old thing; it was the same kind of thing that always happened when Grandpa Rudd and Dad were together, only then Grandpa Rudd was the one *Dad* couldn't win over.

Dad would say, "There's just no pleasing him!"

Dad got so hot under the collar, he didn't even notice Pete pouring me a second glass of wine. I began to get a slight buzz on. It never took much. I began tuning out.

Before dessert was served, Pete had to leave the table and run to the bathroom.

"He had too much to drink," Dad said.

"He's had diarrhea for weeks," Mom said.

"Do we have to hear about it at the table?"

"You never let up on him, Arthur!"

"If he's had diarrhea for weeks, what does my never letting up on him have to do with anything? He shouldn't sock away so many martinis if he's had diarrhea for weeks!"

"He came out here to give us the good news," Mom said. "He was celebrating."

"The time to celebrate is *after* the screenplay sells."

Mom and I groaned.

"Am I being hard on him?" Dad said.

"*You*, Dad?" I said.

"Not *you*," Mom said.

"If I was hard on him, I'm sorry," Dad said.

"Tell *him* that," Mom said.

But when Pete appeared long enough to tell us he was skipping dessert to sack out for a while, Dad said, "Gin will do that."

I figured I had a snowball's chance in hell of getting Dad's apartment the first Saturday in October. I decided not to mention the rock concert. Dad got MTV in New York. He said he only had to watch it five minutes to understand why this entire generation was going to hell in a hand barrel. He'd seen Julie Brown's video "The Homecoming Queen's Got a Gun," and never gotten over it.

"Just you and Jack want to borrow it?" Dad said.

"And our dates."

"No dates," Dad said.

"Dill's mother would never allow that anyway," Mom said.

"She might, Mom. She trusts me."

"You and Jack are welcome," Dad said, "but your dates are not."

"Even if Dill's mother agrees?"

"I'm still responsible," Dad said. "I decline that responsibility, thank you."

After we finished eating, I went up to Pete's room and sat down on his bed. Oscar was sleeping next to him. Oscar really did stink—not only his fur, but his breath, too. Oscar was aging fast.

Both Pete and I had tight, curly red hair. His looked damp, and I put my hand on his forehead. "Are you okay?" He was cold and wet.

"I've been feeling crappy lately. I can't shake that bug I picked up."

While Pete had spent the summer in Europe, I'd stayed in the sublet he had on East Eighteenth Street in New York. Pete had thought I'd like to be independent of Dad, but the truth was I spent most of my time at Dad's place on East Eighty-second Street. I was too lonely at Pete's. I wasn't ever the big reader Pete was. I wasn't the loner he was.

"Do you want to sleep?" I asked him.

"No, stick around."

The wall above Pete's bed featured a montage of Pete sailing, skiing, swimming, surfing. Pete had been a real beach boy when he was my age. Most of the pictures had been taken in the sun. I hated the sun because of the bad burns I'd get, but Pete would burn, peel, go back for more. In some of the pictures his nose, ears, and under his eyes were coated with white sun blocker. Pete was alone in all the pictures but two. He was in one picture with Stan Horton, his boyhood pal and fellow Trekkie. He was in another picture with Michelle Stanton. We'd called her Belle Michelle. She'd been paralyzed after she'd been hit by a wave that damaged her spinal cord, and in that picture Michelle was in her wheelchair. Pete was in her lap, pulling a sun visor down over her eyes, both of them laughing.

"Whatever happened to Belle Michelle?" I asked.

"She got married about a year after Stan married Tina," Pete said. "Tell me about this rock concert you want to go to."

"Dad just said no girls in his apartment. . . . We'll never get tickets anyway."

"Who's Nicki? A new girl?"

"She's Jack's girl. I'd go with Dill."

"Jack's got a steady girl? The Neanderthal Man's making out?"

"Who said anyone was making out? She lives out at Kingdom By The Sea. Nicki Marr's her name."

"Any relation to Annabel Poe Marr?"

"That was her mother."

"I remember Annabel from when *I* worked at the bookstore," Pete said. "She'd always come in for books by Edgar Cayce. Books like *Seth Speaks*. She'd head right for the Occult section. She claimed she was a distant relative of Edgar Allan Poe."

"Her daughter's more down-to-earth," I said. "A little on the fast side."

" 'On the *fast* side'?" Pete hooted. "I didn't think your generation made those crappy value judgments anymore. That sounds more like Dad's generation. I thought we paved the way for you in the seventies, but 'on the fast side' sounds like the fifties all over again. What happened to women's liberation?"

"Dill happened to it," I said. "Dill's even talking about an engagement ring. She says if I'm going to be miles away in another college while she's at Wheaton, I'd better cough up an engagement ring."

"Does she really think that'll stop you?"

"I think she thinks it'll stop her. She says she wants to be a real bride, wear white, and have a real old-fashioned wedding night."

"Oh, one of those. With the groom so twisted on champagne he can't get it up, off somewhere in the mountains with a heart-shaped tub in the bathroom."

We laughed, and Pete gave my arm a sock. "You've got to turn on the charm, Ricky. *'J'ai tant rêvé de toi qu'il n'est plus temps sans doute que je m'éveille.' "*

It was from the same poem that Nicki had mentioned the night before. For a second I felt my blood jump as I remembered Nicki leaning across the table in Sweet Mouth, watching me with her green eyes. . . . "I have dreamed so much of you that it is no longer right for me to awaken."

I said, "Is that the only French poem you know?"

"It's the only one I know you know. . . . Maybe a night in New York is just what you and Dill need."

"Dad's not going to change his mind. You know Dad."

"You can all stay at my place. I'll move out for the weekend. I'll stay with Stan and Tina down in SoHo."

"Would you do that, Pete?"

"Anything to get you laid. Tell Dad the girls are staying someplace else. Tell him you prefer my place because it's nearer all the action."

"I probably won't get laid. I'm not doing a good job of sowing my wild oats before I get married. Dill will probably be the only woman I ever have in my entire life."

"Why don't you play hard to get yourself?" Pete

said. "Give Dill some of her own medicine. Tell her The Neanderthal Man and On the Fast Side can have the bedroom. Tell her you'll sleep in my reclining chair, and she can have the couch. That couch folds out into a bed. You don't have to mention that. . . . Turn the tables on Dill. She'll come around."

"Oh, a new approach. Approach number four thousand and four."

"Try it," Pete urged. "There's someone in my Great Writers' Group who does P.R. work for rock bands. I think I can get you tickets to the Springsteen concert, too."

I couldn't wait to call Dill and tell her.

Four

THE NEXT MORNING Pete was still too sick to drive back to New York with Dad. He was taking the afternoon jitney. Dad said he'd drop me off at school, on his way out of Seaview. That gave him the chance to get on my case about painting the kitchen chairs.

"When you go home for lunch, I want you to speak to Pete about putting Oscar to sleep, too," Dad said as he drove toward Seaview High. "Oscar's too feeble now to enjoy life."

"Pete will never do it. Pete loves that old mutt. So do I."

"That's *why* it should be done. You're doing Oscar a favor."

"Dad? You're always leaning on Pete. If he told you he'd finished *The Skids*, you'd say, Well, it's not published. If he said it was already a screenplay, you'd say, Well, it's not produced yet—the same way you keep telling him Southworth is nowhere."

"Pete doesn't finish what he starts!"

"You didn't let him finish his Ph.D. If you wanted him to be a college professor, you should have let him finish it."

"I would have let him. But I wouldn't pay for it. Pete wasn't working hard at it. Your grandfather paid for four years of my college. I wasted most of those years . . . drinking beer, chasing the girls, sowing *my* wild oats."

I was sitting sideways in the front seat watching him. It was hard to imagine Dad younger, drinking beer and chasing girls.

"I don't see you as the campus make-out artist," I said.

"If I'd stayed one, you mightn't have seen me at all. Ever. I wouldn't have been able to afford a family. Luckily, the money ran out. I paid for my own M.B.A. I took any part-time work I could get. That's when I began to apply myself. Before that I didn't have any discipline. I didn't put any value on education until the money came out of my own pocket."

Pete and I called this rap Rap #2, the Pull Yourself Up by Your Own Bootstraps rap, twin to Rap #3, the Learn the Value of a Dollar rap. Rap #1 was The Family Is First.

"Pete could still get his doctorate, couldn't he?"

"That's what I tried to tell him last night."

"And wouldn't you help him?"

"Erick, Pete hasn't even looked into it. Pete would rather chase off to Paris every summer." Pete hardly ever stayed very long in Paris when he went abroad. He couldn't afford it—he usually earned small grants to go. But Dad invariably described Pete's trips that way, as though Pete was just living it up somewhere dazzling.

"Maybe *The Skids* will bail Pete out," I said.

"Five chapters in nine years? What makes him think he'll write screenplays any faster?" Dad said. "Sometimes I think your brother lives on a pink cloud. He has your mother's cockeyed optimism. Why would he get himself involved in teaching that Great Writers' Discussion Group, free of charge, when he needs money, and he needs time for his own writing?"

"For charitable reasons, maybe? Rain does not fall on one roof alone," I said. It was Mom's favorite saying. It was her justification for being involved in enough good causes to qualify her for sainthood or a nervous breakdown, whichever came first.

"What do you think your mother's most known for around Seaville?" Dad asked me. "Not all the good works she's organized, not *any* of them!"

I knew what he was referring to, and I said, "She can't help that."

"She's most remembered for that fiasco: the Bill Ball!"

She was. True. When her good friend Liz Gaelen's

husband got caught in some Wall Street swindle, and was almost indicted for embezzlement, Mom organized a Bill Ball. All the Gaelens' bills were put into a fishbowl; anyone attending the ball had to pick out a bill and pay it, as the price of admission. Mom got the Seaville Tennis Club to donate the space for the ball. The Gaelens were bailed out of their immediate financial difficulties, but we never heard the end of it. For months letters to the editor in *The Seaville Star* complained that only the rich would dream up such a self-serving celebration.

Dad turned onto School Street. "Pete gets his bleeding-heart ideas from your mother. You know how Pete always was. He was a one-man Salvation Army when he was a kid. Then dating that girl in a wheelchair!"

"But what a girl, Dad! Belle Michelle!"

"Pete was dating her *because* she was in a wheelchair. And I think Michelle was smart enough to know it. I think that's why she threw Pete over. . . . I like your loyalty to Pete, but don't try to be Pete. This ambition of yours to be a writer—that's Pete's ambition. You don't even read. I never see you with a book. At least Pete reads . . . always did."

I jumped at the chance to get Dad off that subject. "Look! Dill!"

"I see her. You've been going with her most of high school, hmmm?"

"I know what you're going to say: Play the field more."

"I like Dill. But now's the time to sow your wild oats. Why so serious with just one girl, Erick?"

She was waiting for me on the front steps of school. She was in jeans, a white shirt, a baggy sweater with the shirt tails hanging out from under it, a loosely knotted tie blowing in the breeze.

"And how do you tell her from a boy?" Dad said.

"Oh, how do you think?" I said.

When Dad laughed, I said, "Hey, Dad, what's that sound you just made?"

"I almost forgot how to make it, after I saw those S.A.T. scores of yours. I hope you're studying those Barron review books I got for you."

"Not to worry, Dad," I said as he stopped the car.

"Not to worry," he said. "That'll be the day."

I held the door open for Dill, and we walked down the hall toward her locker.

When I first met Dill, she always smelled like cookies. I'd tease her about it, and she'd tell me the name of her perfume was Vanilla No. 5. I found out months later that she wasn't kidding. She actually put a few dabs of vanilla extract on every morning.

My mother always said Dill looked so wholesome. That description wasn't exactly a turn-on, but I knew what Mom meant. Dill never needed makeup, never wore much. She had that great clean look the cosmetic ads were always telling females they'd have if they slathered their faces with creams and cover-ups.

"Mom said no to the New York weekend," Dill said. "I didn't even tell her we were going to use Pete's apartment. I said we'd stay at your dad's. She said is Arthur Rudd out of his mind?"

"Maybe *I* should talk to her." I always got along well with Mrs. Dilberto. *Mr.* Dilberto was another matter, second only to my father in his curiosity about my S.A.T. scores, college plans, and the general direction of my next seventeen years.

"It won't do any good to talk to her, honey," Dill said. "I want to go so badly, too, even if it is Nicki Marr's idea."

"Just for Jack's sake, give her a break."

"Why doesn't she give me a break? She looks at me like I'm not there."

"She doesn't know how to socialize."

"With females," Dill said. "I don't even care. I heard Bruce Springsteen sing 'I'm on Fire' last night, and I got goose bumps!"

We were in front of her locker, and she turned around suddenly so that she was pressed against me. "Do you ever get goose bumps?"

"Right now. The size of half dollars."

Dill liked to tease, and I liked her to. Dill said that there was instant coffee, instant tea, and then there was me: instant hots.

"Think of something!" I whispered at her. "We need to get away!"

"I thought all night—there *is* my Aunt Lana in Washington Heights. She's Daddy's kid sister. I think she'd lie for me and say I was staying there. She's *très* romantic."

"Are you *très* romantic?" I asked.

"Are *you*?" Dill said.

"I'm on fire."

Dill turned back to her locker, working the combination while I stepped back to let my blood cool.

"Honey?" Dill said. "If I *do* get Aunt Lana to lie for me, it doesn't mean I'm going to . . ." She didn't finish the sentence. She didn't have to. I knew the end of that sentence by heart.

"Sweetheart," I said, "if you can get her to lie for you, don't worry about that."

"Promise?"

"Promise. Just don't sweat it. Let's just cool out that weekend. We'll give Jack and Nicki the bedroom." I sneaked a look at her expression, to see how that sat with her. I was remembering what Pete had told me. I thought I saw some vague glimmer of regret.

"I'll sleep in Pete's reclining chair. You can have the couch."

Dill flashed me one of her dazzling smiles.

"Super!" she said. "You'd just get horny in the bedroom!"

Five

JACK AND I had a late-Saturday-night tradition. We'd meet at my house and talk until one or two in the morning.

If we double-dated, we'd drop the girls off first. (Dill always had to be in by midnight.) If we didn't double-date, Jack would show up around the same time anyway, tell me about his date, if he'd had one, where they went, what they did. If he hadn't gone on a date, we'd just rap until he left and drove to his house down the street.

Usually *Rock-N-America* or *Music Magazine* was on TV in the background. It was the closest thing to MTV we could get out in Seaville. Jack wasn't at all interested in rock—he barely watched the videos. I was interested, but not hot for them. I only watched them with one eye.

The Saturday night before our New York weekend, Dill and I didn't have a date. She went to Smithtown with her folks, to have dinner at her grandparents'. It was part of her plan to keep her parents in a good mood, so they wouldn't change their minds about New York. Her Aunt Lana had agreed to say that Dill was staying with her in Washington Heights.

Dad and Mom were already in bed by the time I was watching the end of *Saturday Night Live*. I used to love Martin Short on that show, particularly when he played Ed Grimley, the *Wheel of Fortune* freak whose head came to a point. I was sitting there in front of the tube when I heard Jack's car pull up. I was in a great mood. Pete had sent the tickets to the Springsteen concert out with Dad. I couldn't wait to tell Jack.

Jack let himself in the back door. By the time he'd walked through the kitchen and the dining room, I could smell her perfume.

"I brought someone with me," Jack said.

"I see you did. Hi, Nicki."

"Hi, Erick. Is it okay?"

"Sure!" I was barefoot, dressed in an old sweat shirt and sweat pants. There were two empty Coke cans on the coffee table, and wrappers from a Nabisco devil's food cake and a Drake's Yankee Doodles.

Oscar was sleeping in his bed behind the couch. He was so deaf, he didn't hear people come into the house anymore.

Jack was in a sport jacket and a tie, a press in his

gray flannel pants and a shine on his shoes.

Nicki was in this knockout getup: a skinny black-leather skirt, an oversized white T-shirt, a big jeans jacket, a sun-colored scarf the color of her hair, and a couple of wrist chains. She had on fishnet stockings and these sky-high heels.

The usual cigarette hanging on her lips. I had to hustle around and find her an ashtray.

I felt like some kid the grown-ups were visiting, and I hid the cake wrappers under some college catalogs on the coffee table.

Jack said, "We just had dinner with my folks."

"Can I get you some Cokes?"

She shook her head no. Jack said they weren't going to stay.

She said, "Oh, there's Ric Ocasek! I love him!"

Rock-N-America was just coming up on TV.

Jack said, "Maybe I'll get a beer. Is there any out there?"

"There's some Molson's ale. Help yourself."

"You want one?"

"No." Jack knew I rarely drank, that when I did it was always something sweet like a tequila sunrise or a black Russian. Even forgetting Dad's rule that I wasn't to drink until I was the legal age, I didn't like the taste of beer or booze. . . . Jack wasn't a drinker either. He could get bounced from the football team for drinking.

But he went out to the kitchen to help himself.

Nicki asked me if I liked Ric Ocasek too. I told her I hadn't paid much attention to him. I took a look and saw this long-faced, long-haired guy with dark glasses and ears like cup handles.

"I like it that he's so homely," Nicki said, reading my mind. "It takes real nerve to get up and perform when you look like that. He gets better-looking while he's performing, like Dee Snider from Twisted Sister?"

I wasn't crazy about heavy metal, but I remembered one old Twisted Sister video when this kid's father storms into his room and starts calling it a pigsty, calling the kid a slob, asking the kid what he's going to do with his life. "I wanna rock!" the kid tells him, and he throws his father out the window. The kid was Dee Snider; the name of the video was "We're Not Gonna Take It."

Nicki slipped off her high heels and sat with her feet up under her. She started telling me about an interview with Dee Snider that she'd read in the *Newsday Magazine*.

"Dee Snider really did have a father who got after him that way," Nicki said.

I said, "Don't we all."

"One day his father hauled him into a barbershop and made the barber give him this Marine Corps crew cut," Nicki said. "In the interview, his father talked about doing that to him. He said that after, Dee Snider said to him, 'Daddy, I'm tall and skinny. I have a long nose. I have a long jaw. I have braces on my teeth. I have pimples on my face. The only nice thing about me is my hair. And you made me cut it off.' . . . His father felt awful about it."

"It's always too little too late," I said.

I sat beside her on the couch.

She was like a walking encyclopedia on the rock world.

"My favorite song of Ric Ocasek's is 'Jimmy Jimmy,' " she said.

"I don't know it."

"It's real old. It reminds me of *my* daddy, even though it's about a kid. The first verse does, anyway. Daddy's always got to get out. He's restless. Daddy always says we're all in this together, too. There's a line like that in 'Jimmy Jimmy.' "

She leaned forward to touch the cover of one of the college catalogs with her long, slender fingers. I picked up all the catalogs and moved them down the table, so she wouldn't come upon the cake wrappers. "That's just college stuff," I said.

"Where are you going to college?"

"Wherever they'll let me in."

"What do you want to study?"

"Film. I don't know. Writing. Communications."
Communications! I could almost hear Dad's voice. What
the hell does Communications mean? What are *you*
going to communicate? . . . Dad wouldn't be satisfied
until I told him I wanted to study multivariate data
analysis, the globalization of markets, and security and
portfolio management.

"I could go to college if I wanted to," Nicki said,
playing with the cigarette in her mouth, holding it
between her teeth. "Daddy said he'd cash in his sav-
ings bonds so I could."

I had a fleeting vision of him from last summer.
He'd show up at some of the town baseball games,
Lorr's Linoleum playing Diamond's Furniture Store,
those type games. He was a tall, lean, good-looking
fellow with a shock of silver-blond hair that fell across
his brow. He always wore a cap tilted over one eye,
and even though he had this boyish look, the females
he hung out with made him seem like a dirty old man,
because they were always a lot younger, not much
older than Nicki.

"What would you study if you went to college?" I
asked her. Dill wanted to study anthropology and be
another Margaret Mead.

"If I went to college, I wouldn't study," Nicki said.
"I'd play. . . . What I want to do someday?" That was
the way she talked—she said things as though they

were questions. "I want to study fashion? Go to New York City. Study fashion. Or promote rock stars?"

Jack came up behind us and said, "No way! I want you right here with me!" Jack had already decided he was going into business with his father. He said he might take a few courses at Southampton College, but he wanted to settle down in Seaville for the rest of his life. He liked the ocean. He was a surfer like Pete had been. When the weather was warm enough, Jack'd get up and surf before school.

I told them I got the Springsteen tickets. Nicki clapped her hands together, leaned back with her feet off the ground, then came forward and took the cigarette out of her mouth. She threw her arms around me. Her lips glided right past my cheek to my mouth. Her mouth smelled sweet and smoky.

Nicki knew the names of all the performers that came on TV, and all five performers in R.E.O. Speedwagon. She said Kevin Cronin was the best of all, and she knew all the words to his song "The Key." When she sang them very softly for us, Jack kept shaking his head in amazement, giving me these proud looks.

Nicki didn't wear anything like Vanilla No. 5. Her perfume was a different sort from Dill's. It was the kind of perfume that pours out of the ventilators of some department stores on Fifth Avenue. Summer nights in New York sometimes, I'd meet Dad up across from Rockefeller Center, and I remembered the sexy perfumes in the air while I waited, and all the women in flimsy summer dresses, with their legs and arms bare. . . . Something about Nicki reminded me of New York females. Her perfume was serious like theirs. It didn't make you think of cookies.

She told us George O'Dowd was Boy George's real name, and that he was a Gemini like her.

"Like me, too," I said. "I was born May twenty-ninth."

"I was born May twenty-eighth! You know what, Erick? Geminis are *supposed* to be good at communications, so you *should* study Communications! We're communicators! Did you know that?"

She was beginning to communicate something to me, all right.

When she got up to use the downstairs bathroom, just before they left, Jack said, "Do you like her, Erick?"

"What do you keep asking me that for? I keep telling you I like her."

"She's the first girl I ever brought home," Jack said. "Mom took me aside and said, 'Jackie, Jackie, that girl's going to make mincemeat out of you,' but Dad got a kick out of her. Dad trotted out all his old stories about me. Remember that time I put black shoe polish on the ear of the phone in Windmill Deli? Remember all the guys in trucks with their ears black?"

"Are you making out?" I said.

Jack stopped laughing and looked down at the empty bottle of ale. "I feel like I'm twelve years old again, wondering where the noses go when you kiss."

"You were still wondering that when you were fifteen." I laughed.

"Don't remind me. . . . She's used to guys like Ski, and T. X. Hoyle!"

"And Bucky Moon, et cetera, et cetera."

"Not et cetera, et cetera, but I don't think she's ever been with a virgin."

"She doesn't have to know that."

"That's what stops me. I'm afraid she'll be able to tell."

He looked around to see if she was coming up behind him. She wasn't anywhere in sight.

"I think she's gone," he said. He got up.

"Gone where?"

"Out to the car. Sometimes she just disappears. She's always saying, 'Let's go!' right in the middle of things."

"Nice," I said. "Are you supposed to go looking for her?"

"I don't mind," Jack said. "She's not like other girls, Erick. That's what I like about her."

"To each his own," I said. "That's what makes horse races."

"New York's going to change everything," Jack said. "I'm so hot, I'm ready to pop!"

Six

JACK HAD MET Cap Marr, but I never had. Neither had Dill. We were supposed to go to Kingdom By The Sea to meet him the Friday night before we went into New York City. Nicki said he just wanted to look us over, before he let her go off with us for the weekend.

But Cap's manager, Toledo, known around town as the white Mr. T., broke both of Charlie Gilhooley's arms Friday night. Cap had to go and bail him out. Charlie Gilhooley ran The Witherspoon Funeral Home. In Seaville he was known as The Gay Undertaker. He was this tall, sissy blond guy who'd no more make a pass at Toledo than he'd step in front of an oncoming train. But Toledo claimed that was what had happened, in the raunchy Kingdom bar, after Charlie stopped there for a drink after the end of a funeral service in Dune Cemetery.

When we took off early Saturday morning, Toledo

was still in the Seaville jail, waiting for bail to be set.

We picked up Dill first. She hadn't brought along a skirt, much less a dress. When she checked with me about what I was going to wear, I said I wasn't even going to bring a tie, not to a rock concert.

Dill was in skintight Guess? jeans and an Esprit denim jacket, new for the occasion. She had on some Reebok sneakers, and she was carrying a small suitcase with a maroon-and-white Seaville High sticker on the side.

Then we drove out to the ocean for Nicki. She was standing down near the drawbridge to the castle in a wool camp shirt, with a tiny tube skirt and a big, oversized jacket. She had on high heels that sank into the sand under her feet. She was carrying a garment bag with two U2 buttons on it, and another button that said Totally Hot.

The tension in the air between Dill and Nicki was thick enough to cut with a knife. I knew it was all because Dill hated it that Nicki was dressed better than she was. I knew Dill. Whenever we went anywhere, Dill could tell me later what every single female had on, with all the detail you'd see under some ad in a fashion magazine.

Dill wasn't saying much. Dill never had to. She was giving off the kinds of vibes that make water into ice.

Nicki wasn't one to take that kind of thing lying

down, either. She said something about what a sweet little suitcase that was on the floor in back—"somebody has real school spirit, too"—and she was smoking like a fiend, while Dill waved away the smoke with her hands and rolled the back window all the way down.

Dill kicked things off by saying something about poor Charlie; how could anyone have let that happen? Jack said Charlie finally got what he was asking for.

We were all used to Charlie in Seaville. He wasn't a macho gay like some of the ones who came out to Seaville on weekends and in summer. You could tell what Charlie was by looking at him, and if you heard him talking behind you in a restaurant, you could tell what Charlie was. Charlie never asked for anything but to be left alone with his embalming fluids and his funeral processions. I think most of us in Seaville had the kind of affection for Charlie any small town has for one of its characters. He was our resident gay.

Nicki said, "Don't stick up for Toledo just because of me, Jack. See, Toledo's afraid if fairies hang out at the bar, they'll ruin business, what little we've got."

"The story is that Charlie sidled up to Toledo and said, 'Hi, thweeheart,' and Toledo belted him really hard," Jack said.

"Oh, sure," I said, "that sounds just like Charlie."

"Let me tell you the story that's going around, okay?"

Jack said. "After Toledo belted Charlie, he picked Charlie up and threw him out the door. When Toledo started to walk away, Charlie managed to get himself up on one elbow. 'Yoo hoo,' Charlie called out to Toledo, 'I forgive you.' "

"That's a crappy joke," I said.

"It didn't happen that way at all," said Nicki. "See, once they start coming into a place, then others follow, that's what Daddy says, so Toledo asked him to leave before he even served him. But Charlie wouldn't."

"I'm just trying to make a joke of it," Jack said. "You know: What do you call a gay bar without bar stools? A fruit stand."

Dill thought that was funny, and she laughed, finally.

She leaned against me and whispered, "Honey? Do you think you'll ever laugh at anything again?"

I whispered back, "Sweetheart? When you don't ever have sex, your muscles freeze in one position, making it impossible to laugh."

"Tough tuna, Rudd!" Dill said.

We got to Pete's place about eleven in the morning. It was on Eighteenth Street, on the second floor of an old brownstone. Pete was subletting it from some professor on sabbatical in London.

Right away Jack said he and Nicki wanted to sleep

in the living room that night. Nicki'd like to fall asleep to MTV, and since it was my brother's place, Dill and I should have the bedroom. I knew old Jack. The first thing he did when we parked out at Montauk Point on double dates was turn up the music loud.

Dill and I were due at her Aunt Lana's, in Washington Heights, for lunch. Dill said Aunt Lana wanted to meet the reason she had to lie.

Nicki turned on MTV first thing.

Cyndi Lauper was singing her old song "She Bop."

"I love this thing!" Nicki said.

"Do you know what it's about?" Dill said. "Yeck!"

"It's just about masturbation," Nicki said.

"It is?" I said.

Dill made another face and Nicki laughed. She was sitting on a pillow on the floor, in front of the TV, blowing smoke rings.

She said, "Cyndi Lauper's neat because her mother's in nearly all her videos. Besides, she's a Gemini, like Erick and me."

"Time to get to work!" Jack called out.

We'd agreed to eat our dinner in, to save money, and Jack and Dill got busy in Pete's small kitchen: Dill fixing a meat loaf for later, Jack concentrating on something he called Long Island Tea, a drink he said we'd all have a little of after the Springsteen concert, to celebrate his birthday.

I kept Nicki company in the living room.

"I never hung out with a crowd before," Nicki said.

"I never hung out without one," I said.

"Mostly I was with Ski. Did you know Ski?"

"I'd see him roaring around on his Kawasaki. I'd see you hanging on for dear life on the back."

"I loved going on that thing!" She was rolling the cigarette around between her teeth that way she had of doing.

"Weren't you ever afraid of breaking your neck?" I asked her.

"I was never afraid of anything with Ski. I was more afraid of going to Jack's house for dinner."

"But you had a good time?"

"My idea of having a good time? It isn't having everyone look me over to see if I measure up. I hate all that family-around-the-table crap!"

"Whatever happened to Ski, anyway?"

"He was busted for dealing. If your name's Walter Ruski, you get sent up when you break the law. If your name's Richard Gaelen, somebody throws your wife a Bill Ball to get her out of debt."

I raised my hands like she was sticking me up. "Richard Gaelen's married to my mother's best friend," I said sheepishly.

"And he's a crook!" Nicki said.

"He beat the rap," I agreed.

Nicki leaned back on her hands, smoke curling up past her face. "See, Jack takes me home to meet his folks. He wants me to get along with his friends. That's the way it should be, I suppose. But it isn't the way it really is, any more than I'd ever be a real pom-pom girl, even if those bitches had voted me in! I'm coming from somewhere else. I'm not like them. I don't want to be, either."

"If you don't want to be like them, don't sweat it."

"I want to be better than them. I want to be like Cyndi Lauper. She stayed what she is, and turned out better than all the ones who thought *they* were better."

"The rock world is full of yesterday's losers," I said.

"Yesterday's, right. Look at them now."

"Didn't you go through all the family-around-the-table crap with Ski?"

"I knew his family from hanging out with him, but no big deal."

"How about with T. X.?"

"T. X.? You've got to be kidding!"

"Bucky?"

She was shaking her head no, vigorously, as though I was asking her something crazy like where the million dollars was buried.

"I guess I'm used to real riffraff, only after one thing," she said. "And I don't mean Jack. I know Jack's not that way."

I wasn't going to touch that one with a ten-foot pole.

I said, "Riffraff's a word my mother'd use."

"My mother used to say it, too. My mother used to say, 'Nicki, don't let anyone treat you like riffraff, because a famous psychic once told me that I was royalty in another life.'"

That made me laugh. We were both laughing when Dill came out of the kitchen and said it was time to go to Aunt Lana's.

Just before we left, I went into the small bathroom, and Jack pushed his way in with me. "What time are you coming back?"

"How do I know?"

"Give me a time!"

"Four o'clock. Okay?"

Then I said, "Jack? She just finished telling me she's used to guys only after one thing, but you're not that way."

"Well, I am that way. She never dates anyone who isn't."

"Maybe you shouldn't pounce on her first thing."

"When am I going to pounce on her? Tonight? With you guys right in the next room?"

"Maybe you just shouldn't pounce."

"Why shouldn't I?"

On the wall over Jack's head was Pete's old framed drawing of Mr. Spock from *Star Trek*. Spock was glanc-

ing wistfully at a woman, with the caption underneath:
BUT LOVE? LOVE IS ILLOGICAL.

I was thinking that if Jack really loved her, he'd have a little more finesse. He wouldn't try to pin her to the mat first chance.

"Everyone she's ever been with has pounced," I said.

"That's just why I *should*. She's going to think something's wrong with me."

"She's not going to think that." I didn't know why it should bother me.

"I'm going to think it, too," Jack said. "I'm not you, Erick. I'm not into waiting now that I've met someone I'm crazy about! I'm eighteen now, for God's sake!"

Then he gave my arm a punch and said, "Wish me luck!"

Seven

ONE THING I could never say to anyone was I love you, not even to Dill. I'd say "Love ya!" I'd sign notes "Lots of love," and send Hallmark cards with mushy verses, but I could never get those three words out.

Pete said not to worry about it—even Dad managed to choke them out when he met Mom. You'll say them in time, Pete said, maybe not to Dill but when you're ready. I'd tell him I'm ready now, and not being able to say them makes me come off a wimp. The other thing, I told Pete, is that I hate watching TV or going to the movies with Dill when some character says I love you, because I always think Dill's wondering why I don't. She does, but I don't.

I was thinking about all of that while Dill and I were in Washington Heights, visiting her Aunt Lana.

It was a fantastic early-fall afternoon, the kind of Saturday that makes you think of football games, that smells like leaves burning even when leaves aren't burning anywhere, cool enough for sweaters, but not cold enough for gloves or coats.

We rode the bus up Madison Avenue, and when we passed 90th Street, I told her that was where South-worth School was, where Pete taught.

"Sometimes I look at Pete, and think that's what you're going to look like and be like when we're married," Dill said. "It's like seeing into the future."

"The last thing I'd do is teach, though. It's the last thing anyone'd let me do, too."

"You could teach if you wanted to. You can do anything Pete can do."

"When I was a kid, I used to worry that I could never be as good as Pete at anything."

"All kid brothers think that," Dill said. "But you're already like Pete. You have his sense of humor, and you have his high moral character, and you have his hard buns." She gave me a pinch. She said, "Now for my side of the family, and our black sheep. She's the only Dilberto who ever eloped!"

The last thing you'd think when you looked at Dill's Aunt Lana was that once she'd run off with a Spanish guitarist from the Bronx, named Gustavo Quintero.

She was this little, bespectacled music teacher with blue eyes like Dill's, and wiry gray hair, cut short and on the frizzy side. The only clue to her infamous past was all the little guitar-shaped bric-a-brac strewn about her small apartment: guitar-shaped napkin rings, ashtrays, bookends, and pencil holders.

She looked a lot younger than Mr. Dilberto, and the thing I liked best about her was the fact she didn't like him any more than I did. She called him Bertie, and said that if you kicked him in the heart, you'd break your toe.

"Oh, Aunt Lana!" Dill said. "You really love Daddy deep down!"

"If you mean my love for him is buried in the debris of bygone years, you're right, Dill. . . . I can just imagine what you're going through. Bertie doesn't think God is good enough to date a Dilberto. And who are we? Just some offspring of Venetian cobblers who got off the boat like everyone else in the dear old U.S. of A. . . . What fault does he find with you, Erick?"

We were eating chicken salad in her small foyer.

"He thinks I ought to be applying to Harvard or Yale."

"Or Princeton or blah blah," she said. "That's Bertie."

"Erick?" Dill said. "You're exaggerating."

"Bertie's bite is worse than his bark, too," said Aunt Lana. "The man I fell in love with couldn't read or write. You can imagine what Bertie made of that."

"That *was* awful," Dill agreed. "I heard that story.

Daddy pretended he'd left his reading glasses home, and passed a menu to Gustavo and asked Gustavo what the day's specials were."

Aunt Lana said, "I was suspicious when he asked us out to dinner, said, C'mon, Lana, let your big brother treat you and your new beau. I knew right then Bertie was up to something. . . . I'll tell you kids something: People are small sometimes. Puny. They say they're doing things for your own good, but all they're doing is reinforcing the pettiness in their own natures. They can't seem to just thank the Lord they're doing okay in life. They've got to try and make everything in your life the way they think it should be. If it isn't, if it can't be, if you don't want it to be, that never stops them. . . . Bertie always started every sentence 'If I were you, Lana . . .' And I'd say, 'But you're not! No one can be *me* but *me*!' . . . If Bertie was God, everyone's fingerprints would be exactly the same."

Dill tried to change the subject a few times. I don't think she'd counted on the tirade against her father. I felt a little sorry for her, too. Even though I had no love for Mr. Dilberto, I knew what it was like to feel no better than one of Hitler's relatives, suddenly. After my mother's grand Bill Ball for Liz Gaelen I felt that way, too, when I read all the letters of outrage in *The Seaville Star*.

By the time we were ready to leave, I realized Aunt

Lana had the idea Dill and I were these endless-love type star-crossed lovers, right up there with Romeo and Juliet.

As she was seeing us out the door, she said, "If Bertie calls here tonight, I'll say you're out if it's early, and you're in the shower if it's late. Then I'll call you so you can call him." Behind her there was a sampler on the wall, in the shape of a guitar, with these words inside it:

> She said, Give fate a good fight, anyway,
> Give chance an argument for us.
> She said, Give fate a good fight, anyway—
> What have we got but us, Gus?
> —from a song by Gustavo Quintero.

When we left, Dill told me she used to write down all the songs he made up—"Daddy said she'd sit there nights taking them down like he was another Billy Joel, always in these awful roadhouses where he'd play."

"What became of him?"

"After they were married about six years, Daddy decided to welcome Gustavo into the family and stop all his criticizing of him. Daddy missed seeing Lana was why. . . . About a year after that Gustavo went out for a pack of cigarettes one day and never came back. I'm glad *you* don't smoke."

"She had her big romance, anyway."

"Sometimes I think Daddy made it possible. Daddy says nothing fans the flames of love like someone forbidding it." Dill bumped against me and smiled. "Are we having our big romance?"

"I am," I said. "Are you?"

"I am if you are."

But the easy little games Dill and I played together came harder somehow. I'd suggested we walk up to the Cloisters, we were so near there. As we went up the dirt path through Fort Tryon Park, I kept thinking that Dill and I weren't even close to being what her aunt thought we were. Dill and I were just kids playing around.

I kept thinking about Jack and Nicki, too, and what was going on back at Pete's place.

The first time I'd ever gone to the Cloisters, Mom had taken me. It was a museum of medieval art, overlooking the Hudson River. The grounds were beautiful, but I never got turned on by old paintings and tapestries, as Mom did, as Pete did, too. Mom said someday I would, the same thing Pete said about saying I love you. While Dill raved over everything we saw, and I pretended to be just as fascinated, I began to wish I'd grow up.

Later we sat on a stone bench, with a light breeze blowing off the river, and Dill said, "Why do you keep looking at your watch?"

"Do I keep looking at my watch?"

"Oh, I get it. We're not supposed to be back to Eighteenth Street until a certain hour. What hour?"

"Four o'clock. We can get started. The bus takes a while."

We got up and began walking along slowly.

"I feel like I should apologize," Dill said.

"For what?"

"For not being a little slut like Nicki Marr."

"I guess you can't make a sow's ear out of a silk purse," I said. . . . "How come it's okay for Jack to make out, but she's a little slut?"

Dill let that one go by.

Dill said, "What were you laughing so hard at when I came out of the kitchen this morning?"

"Something her mother said once."

"You should have seen your face."

"What was wrong with my face?"

"Nothing. You looked wildly happy."

On the bus Dill said, "Did you ever hear how Annabel Poe Marr died?"

"No, I don't know much about Nicki."

"It's a sad story. I could feel sorry for her if she'd ever let anyone female feel *anything* for her."

"What happened to her mother?"

"Jeannie Gaelen's mother was selling Mrs. Marr some of her wardrobe. It was right around the time Jeannie's father got into that trouble. Only no one in Seaville knew it yet. They needed money desperately.

A lot of women get money selling their clothes to Annabel's Resale Shop. They don't admit it, but I could name you names."

"And?"

"And Mrs. Marr always went to the estates to buy the clothes. No one ever wants to be seen in that shop. It's a dead giveaway that you're hard up. Annabel Poe was this sickly type, anyway, among other things. Sickly, psychic: She used to conduct seances on the dunes at Kingdom By The Sea. . . . She had a bad heart. She had a heart attack while she was at the Gaelens'. . . . Instead of calling an ambulance for her, Jeannie's mother called Cap. You know why she didn't call an ambulance? She didn't want it to get around that she was doing business with Mrs. Marr. That's the only reason Mrs. Marr would have been out at the Gaelen estate."

"Pretty," I said.

"I know. Jeannie feels terrible about it. . . . Nobody could find Cap right away. He got there about an hour and a half later. Annabel Poe died on the way to the hospital, in the Kingdom pickup truck."

"Really pretty."

"Jeannie was going to vote Nicki into pom-pom just because of that."

"Well, why not? I would have, too."

"You can't vote someone into pom-pom just because you're sorry for her."

"What would have been so bad about Nicki being a pom-pom girl?"

"She's not pom-pom material. She doesn't have the right school spirit."

"What difference does all that crap make?"

"The difference between a good pom-pom team and a bad one," Dill said. . . . "I don't think she's all that crazy about Jack, either. I'm picking up something else."

"Like what?"

"Like the way she watches you. Like the way she raved over the picture of you and Pete, on Pete's desk, and said there was something about redheaded men that could open up her soul and let out the demon. Did you hear *that* one?"

"That's just something she got from an old R.E.O. Speedwagon song. She was singing it for Jack and me last Saturday."

"I don't care where it was from, she wasn't saying it about Jack. And what about Oh! Cyndi Lauper's a Gemini," Dill tried imitating Nicki, "like Erick and me?"

I just shut up.

"If she likes 'She Bop' so much, she must play with herself, too."

"Who doesn't?" I said. "At least she isn't limited to that."

"Oh, thanks, Rudd!" Dill said.

*   *   *

After we got off the bus at Eighteenth Street and started walking toward Pete's brownstone, Dill said, "Shall we knock first or just barge in?"

"Jack knows we're coming back at four. It's ten after."

But we both made a lot of noise going up the stairs.

I punched the bell a few times, put my key in the lock, and opened the door.

Dill was right behind me. I heard her suck in her breath when we got inside, and whisper, "Oh, no!"

The three of them were sitting in the living room: Jack, Nicki, and my father.

Dad said, "It's all right, Erick."

It didn't look all right. Jack's face was down to his shoes, and Nicki sat staring at her hands folded in her lap.

Dad got up. It was the first time I'd ever seen him wearing old pants and a sweater in New York City.

I said, "Is Mom okay?" It was the only reason I could think of for his being there, that something had happened to Mom.

"She's fine. Mom's fine," Dad said. "But Pete's little virus landed him in St. Vincent's hospital last night. I think they'll let him come home later. So why don't you kids come to my place?"

Dad had known that Jack and I were staying at Pete's, but I'd told him Dill and Nicki were staying at Dill's aunt's.

I think Dad had figured things out for himself, because as we were all getting our stuff together, he never once asked the girls if they had anything to get from Washington Heights.

Dill babbled away guiltily about how lucky we were to get to stay in his beautiful apartment, as we taxied there.

"Yes," said Dad, "but you're going to have to put up with me. . . . I'll give you girls the bedroom, though."

I was sitting up front with the driver. I didn't dare turn around to see the expression on Dill's face, Jack's, or Nicki's.

Eight

I NEVER WATCHED anyone perform without seeing myself doing the same thing. I suppose if I'd been watching Boy George that night, I'd be picturing myself wearing a wig, or red eyeglasses and lipstick, doing those loopy steps he did. But I was seeing myself as Bruce Springsteen. I was imagining myself after a few months without shaving, a red-and-white bandana wrapped around my forehead, my hair longer, and an old T-shirt with the short sleeves rolled, stained with sweat, sticking to my back.

By the time he got around to doing his old hit "Born in the U.S.A.," the sweat was pouring off him and he looked supermacho, punching the air with his fists, flexing his muscles. . . . I was already planning to work out.

Most of the time we stood on our seats. Half of me was as high as anyone there wired on coke or pot or 'faced on booze, but the other half of me was thinking the same thoughts I'd had all day: that there was something lacking in me, that I ought to change. I couldn't seem to leave myself behind, even for Springsteen.

I couldn't seem to leave Nicki behind, either.

I'd done a double take the second she'd stepped out of Dad's bedroom. She had on these black fishnet tights with an orange dress over them. Tipped forward on her head was one of these porkpie jobs in black leather. But it was the black-leather fringe jacket that got to me. There was a picture of a white Corvette slamming into a red Porsche, with other sleek sports cars rammed into each other behind it, white stars shooting out above it. Under that in yellow were the words: TRAFFIC ACCIDENT.

She'd said Ski'd found it for her.

"What's it supposed to mean?" I asked her.

"It's just a traffic accident, see?"

I kept watching her all through the concert.

If anyone knew how to enjoy a rock concert, Nicki did. She stood on her seat mesmerized when Bruce Springsteen sang songs like "I'm on Fire," then jumped down and danced in the aisles to numbers like "Thunder Road," and "Dancing in the Dark." She sang, whistled, shouted, squealed, and clapped.

Jack was trying hard to whip himself up, sneaking sips of Long Island Tea he'd brought along in a flask, wearing a Sting T-shirt Nicki'd given him for his birthday. Dill was excited, but Dill excited was Dill grinning broadly and grabbing my hand—nothing ever completely totaled Dill.

The three of us seemed like grown-ups who'd brought a kid along to the circus, only Nicki wasn't a kid—one whiff of her perfume told you that, one glimpse of her long legs moving to the beat, a rhinestone bracelet flashing at one ankle.

We were all really pooped after, and in the taxi on the way back to Dad's, I asked Jack what was in that tea, anyway. He was sitting there singing Elvis Presley's old torcher "Can't Help Falling in Love," Springsteen's first encore. Jack was doing sort of a slow, dopey version of it, keeping time with his hands.

"Have some and see." He offered me the flask.

"Erick?" Dill said. "It isn't tea. I was there this morning when Jack made it."

"I know it isn't tea, but what's in it? Is it strong?"

"Is it strong!" Nicki said, but she'd had only a taste. None of us were drinkers.

"It's got tequila, rum, vodka, gin, Triple Sec, and lemon juice in it," Dill said.

"And Coca-Cola," Jack said. "You just sip a little of it. Have some!"

I passed. We all did but Jack. Dad had put the kibosh on that part of the celebration. Even though he'd said he was going to stay out late so we could have the apartment to ourselves for a while, I didn't dare get wrecked anywhere around him. . . . I didn't know how to figure Dad's mood. He didn't seem at all teed off at the fact the girls' luggage was at Pete's. All he wanted was our promise not to hang out after the concert. Pick up a pizza on the corner of Eighty-second and Second, he'd said. I'll see you tomorrow, or if you're up very late, later.

We stopped for the pizza. (We'd left the meat loaf in Pete's refrigerator.)

While Jack and I were paying for the pizza at the counter, I said, "When did my old man show up?" We hadn't had a chance to talk since that morning.

"Nicki and I took a walk, because as soon as you and Dill left, Nicki started talking about going back to Seaville right away. She always wants to go when she gets anyplace. I got her calmed down, but he was there when we got back from the walk, around three."

"Sorry, old buddy."

"Don't be. It wouldn't have been the right time anyway. She wanted to see Springsteen so damn much, then she pulls this 'let's go' shit! I can't figure her out. She says she hates to stay till the end of anything."

"She sounds bananas to me," I said, and I noticed Jack lurching.

"This girl's got me on a roller coaster. I'm flying!"

"You're flying, all right. Why are you drinking?"

"No Coach Paul lectures, please."

"Coach Paul would have your ass if he could see you now."

"I feel great!" Jack said.

"Do you know what I'm saying, Jack? You're not really irresistible when you drink. You sing off-key, too."

"Do you know what *I'm* saying? I'll probably marry this girl!"

"Now you're going to marry her." I didn't want to hear about it. "What'd you all talk about for an hour, while you were waiting for Dill and me?"

"College. S.A.T.s. Your dad said I really ought to go to college, and he got Nicki saying the same thing. I kept thinking at the concert, maybe I ought to go."

"Then go!" I said.

"It's a crazy idea, just when I meet someone I don't ever want to leave. What college could I get in?"

"Shit, Jack!"

"Don't say shit Jack! What college could I get in?"

"What college can *I* get in? When we get back to Seaville, we'll talk about it. You're not in control, buddy."

"I love her, Erick. She says we have to be careful today, because it's the fifth and five is a mystic number that means trouble."

"Don't have any more, okay? Dad's going to break

my butt if you're drunk when he gets back."

Dad's apartment consisted of a bedroom, a bathroom, a study, and a kitchen off the living room. I figured Dad could sleep on the couch in his study, Jack on the living-room couch, me on some pillows from the couch on the living-room floor.

It was Dill's idea to change for bed, then eat the pizza in the living room, watching MTV.

Since Jack and I didn't have anything to change into (we slept in our shorts) we put the pizza out on the coffee table and found some paper plates up in Dad's cupboard.

Dill came out of the bedroom first, wearing a pair of her dad's old striped pajamas with the sleeves and pants rolled up.

I cornered her in the kitchen. "Jack's still drinking."

"I'd drink, too, if she was my date for a birthday weekend. Didn't she think of a cake? Some candles we could put on top of the pizza? Something?"

"She gave him the T-shirt," I said.

"That thing will fall apart in the wash," Dill said. "She wouldn't wear it herself. Have you noticed the clothes she's brought along for herself this weekend?"

Right on cue, Nicki came out of the bedroom in a silk robe that looked like it was torn at the bottom, with something white and silk and torn-looking under it. Barefoot, the same rhinestone ankle bracelet. The white lace scarf she'd worn around her neck to the concert was holding back her long blond hair.

We sat around gobbling down pizza and watching MTV, but the fun was gone out of the evening for Dill, who looked like a little boy over on Dad's couch. Nicki spread herself out on the rug, leaning back against a pillow, blowing perfect smoke rings up at the ceiling. The Long Island Tea was beginning to show on Jack. He was stretched out on the rug, too, on his back, trying to talk with his eyes closed, close to konking out.

Dad's apartment always looked like the maid just left, and I was running around after we ate, getting the pizza carton and the paper plates ready to carry down to the incinerator.

Dill came into the kitchen and said, "All she needs is a feather boa wrapped around her neck. I feel like some eighth grader still going through my tomboy stage."

"What the hell am I going to do about Jack when Dad gets here?"

"Leave Jack where he is. I'll get her to bed. Let's just start all over tomorrow. Okay?"

I kissed her. I said, "Do you want to take a walk in Central Park tomorrow morning? Early?"

"Just the two of us, please," Dill said.

I kissed her again. I could hear Nicki in the background saying, "Jack? Wake up!" I knew she'd never wake him up if he'd passed out.

I could hear Honeymoon Suite singing their old song about a hot summer night and a new girl.

"Nicki?" Dill called in. "Bedtime. Okay?"

"Okay," she called back. "Go ahead and use the bathroom first."

I took everything down to the incinerator.

When I came back, Nicki was standing in the kitchen. I could hear the water running in the bathroom down the hall.

"I can't wake Jack up," Nicki said. She leaned against the refrigerator and watched me. "What did you like best in the concert?"

" 'Thunder Road,' I guess. I like that bit he does at the end, on his knees, when he slides across to the saxophonist."

"I like 'Born in the U.S.A.' best," Nicki said. "That part about the woman his brother loved in Saigon? About him having a picture of his brother in her arms?"

I kept smelling that perfume of hers.

She said, "I liked 'Dancing in the Dark,' too. I wouldn't mind being asked to dance with him like that girl was tonight? He did the same thing on the video, asked a girl from the audience up onstage."

"Nicki," I said, "Jack doesn't usually drink."

"I don't care if somebody drinks. Ski drank."

"I just wanted you to know that."

"It's how somebody drinks."

"That's why he isn't drinking well. He doesn't drink."

"He doesn't drink well, and he doesn't let me talk about things. I can't even mention Ski's name."

"Jack's jealous. You can't blame him."

"But I like to talk about things. I can, with you." She had her arms folded in front of her, her head cocked to one side, eyes watching me that way, one eyebrow raised.

I heard Dill call, "Good night," as she came out of the bathroom.

"Good night," I called back.

"Tell Nicki the bathroom's free."

"She's trying to wake Jack up to say good night," I said.

And Nicki smiled.

"Is that what I'm doing?" she said softly.

"I just said that so she wouldn't think . . ." I didn't have a finish for it.

I heard the bedroom door shut.

"So she wouldn't think what?" Nicki said.

"Whatever you girls think," I mumbled.

We were inches away from each other.

"See, I'm not one of the girls," Nicki said.

"I know you're not." I thought she could probably see my heart coming through my shirt.

I turned around to get a glass of water I didn't even want, just to do something with my hands besides put them on her.

"It's funny, because I never thought you liked me," she said.

"I like you fine." I could hardly hear my own words.

"I know you do, now."

I thought I heard her say my name, but I wasn't sure. I kept running the water.

Then she touched my shoulder.

"Hey? Erick?"

"What?"

I turned around. I felt her arms reach up to my shoulders and I just gave in. I felt silk. I felt the soft wetness of her mouth, and the warm rush of my blood.

"Hello? It's me!" I heard Dad's voice in the foyer. "Where is everyone?"

I let go of her.

"In the kitchen, Dad!"

Then we turned around, and Dad was standing there with the Sunday *Times* under his arm.

"Hi, Mr. Rudd! How's Pete?" Nicki said.

"Pete's fine!" Dad said. "How was the concert?"

I didn't even attempt to wake up Jack. Jack was the last person I wanted to face right then, anyway.

Nicki said good night and disappeared into the bedroom.

It was past one in the morning. Dad usually went to bed around eleven.

I told him I'd sack out in the living room with Jack, figuring Dad couldn't wait to get into his study and hit the couch.

But Dad surprised me by getting down a glass, getting out some ice cubes, and splashing some scotch over them.

"I'm going to have a drink, Erick. Come into the study with me."

I didn't like the tone of his voice, or the set of his shoulders, squared way back beyond the posture for Raps #1, #2, or #3. Something told me I'd been a jackass to think Dad would ever let me get away with lying about where the girls were staying that weekend. Not Dad. He just wasn't going to chew me out in front of the others. Dad could always bide his time.

I watched him run his hands over his nearly bald head as I walked behind him into the study. I stood there while he set down his glass and said, "Shut the door."

I shut it, and we both sat down. He sat in the big leather Eames chair, and I sat across from him on the couch.

I thought, Here it comes.

I could still feel where her lips had touched mine, and smell her perfume. We could still hear the faint sounds of MTV pumping away in the living room.

I looked from the shag rug to the framed photographs of Pete and me, taken on Pete's graduation day. (I was in my first suit, standing on tiptoe so I could get my two fingers up behind Pete's head to make horns.) Finally, I looked over at Dad's face, which was as grim and stony as I'd ever seen it.

I started mumbling something about being sorry for the lie. I got the idea anything I was going to come up with was going to be shot down in a second.

"Let *me* talk," Dad said.

I looked down at my Nikes and waited

"Pete's sick," Dad said. "Pete's very ill."

I felt that silly sort of relief I used to feel when I was a kid and Pete was getting hell for something I had nothing to do with. Then the words "very ill" began registering.

"How ill?"

"Erick, anything we say has to be between us. I want that understood."

"All right."

"You're not to talk about this with Jack, or Dill, or that other one. You're not to discuss this with *anyone*! Is that clear?"

"Yes. But what's Pete got?"

It took him a long time to say it. "AIDS. . . . I think you know what AIDS is?"

I'd heard dozens of jokes about AIDS. (What do the letters GAY stand for? "Got AIDS yet?" . . . Did you hear about the new disease gay musicians are coming down with? BAND-AIDS. . . . What do you call a faggot in a wheelchair? ROLLAIDS.) I remembered they'd touched on AIDS briefly in health class. Mostly gay men got it. Some drug addicts got it, too.

"How could Pete get *that*?" I said. I remembered something about people getting it from blood transfusions. I remembered Pete always gave blood during the Red Cross drives. But how could you get it *giving* blood?

Dad was taking a gulp of his scotch, putting the glass down, crossing and uncrossing his legs.

"Erick," Dad said, "we have to think about Pete now."

"That's who I am thinking about!"

Dad put his hand up to hush me.

"We just have to think about Pete. We're not going to judge him. We're going to support him."

"Okay," I said impatiently. "Okay." But I'd caught the word "judge."

So I sat there, waiting for Dad to continue.

"Apparently," Dad began, "your mother is the only one in the family who really knows Pete well."

Nine

"I GUESS I really screwed up your weekend," Pete said as he let me in the door the next morning.

"It was headed in that direction anyway," I said.

At noon I was meeting Jack, Dill, and Nicki at the Central Park Zoo. Then we were going to walk up Fifth Avenue to the Metropolitan Museum of Art. Dill'd heard there was a pool with fountains in there, where we could all have lunch. . . . I hadn't even met Nicki's eyes that morning.

I'd said only that Pete had picked up the virus he'd had in France last summer, that I was going to take him a Sunday *Times* and stay with him for a while.

"You want some coffee, don't you?" Pete said. He walked into the kitchen to pour us some. "How was the Springsteen concert?"

I left the *Times* on the hall table. I described the mob scene at Madison Square Garden, Springsteen's raps between numbers, and how he'd finally wound up doing John Fogerty's "Rockin' All Over the World" as his last encore. . . . I told Pete to thank whoever it was in his Great Writers' Discussion Group for getting us the tickets.

Pete had his back to me. He was getting cream from the refrigerator and sugar from the cupboard. "It's the *Gay* Writers' Discussion Group," Pete said. "Last night Dad said what do you discuss? I said we discuss gay books. Dad said is a gay book a book that sleeps with other books of the same sex?"

Pete laughed, so I did, too.

He looked even thinner than when I'd last seen him. He had on rust-colored corduroys, a white shirt, old Nikes, no socks.

"Dad can't stand the word 'gay,' " Pete said. "When he hears it, his face squishes up like a bird dropped something white out of itself down on Dad."

We were both smiling while we carried the mugs of coffee into the living room and sat down. Pete had The Phil Woods Quartet on. He loved jazz, Charlie Parker, Gerry Mulligan. Anything I knew about jazz I'd learned from Pete.

He crossed his legs and looked over at me with a shake of his head, said, "Well, Ricky, this is sort of a variation on that joke about the gay guy trying to convince his mother he's really a drug addict. You've probably heard it."

"Or one like it," I said. The jokes I'd heard were never about "gay guys." They were always about "fags," "fruits," worse.

"How's Dad taking this?" Pete asked me. "I couldn't really tell."

"He's worried about your health. I am, too."

"I don't mean my health."

"I think he's hurt."

"Because I told Mom I'm gay but not him, hmmm?"

"Yeah."

"And you, pal? I was planning to tell you."

"When I grew up, or what?"

"I don't blame you for being pissed off, Ricky. I was waiting for the right time."

"You act like you had a crime to confess or something. I'm not Dad, Pete. I told Dad last night: It's just another way of being. It's not a crime. It's not anything to be ashamed about."

Pete got up to play the other side of the tape. "I thought you sort of knew anyway."

"How would I sort of know?" I said. "You sort of know about someone like Charlie Gilhooley, but how would I sort of know about you?"

Pete went back and sat down. "I never brought any women home. I never talked about any women. I'm twenty-seven years old."

"You talked about going out to discos, dancing all night."

"Yeah, I guess I did. I didn't say they were gay discos."

"What about Belle Michelle?"

"That was ten or eleven years ago," Pete said. "Michelle always knew about me. I never tried to fool *her*. I didn't want her to think the reason I didn't make any passes had anything to do with her."

"We always thought she was your big love. Dad thought she threw you over and you never got over it."

"Michelle and I were just great pals, at a time when we both needed pals. She was in her wheelchair, and I was in my closet." Pete smiled. "Michelle said as long as I stayed in my closet, she'd understand perfectly if I parked my car in a handicapped space, too."

"So when did you tell Mom?"

"Right before I went to Europe last summer."

"Dad made it sound like she'd always known."

"Maybe she did, deep down—I don't know. . . . Getting up the courage to tell Mom was the hardest thing I ever had to do," Pete said. "How many times have you heard Mom say we were the perfect family? She and Dad never played around on each other, never even had a fight that lasted overnight . . . and while all their friends' kids were raising every kind of hell, we were the good boys. We didn't do drugs, or drink, or cheat in school, or wrap the family car around trees."

"You came close," I said.

"I got a few speeding tickets."

"I know what you mean, though," I said. "Mom always thought we were the Waltons, or the Lawrences on *Family*."

"My God, the Lawrences!" Pete winced. "I forgot how Mom loved to watch the Lawrences: Buddy and Willy and Kate and Jim, et cetera, happy ever after in that big blue house, wrapping up every problem from adultery to abortion in sixty minutes flat, with time out for commercials."

"She still watches the reruns," I said. "Yeah, I always thought *I* was going to be the one to blot the family record."

Pete chuckled. "Not your big brother, hmmm?"

"I didn't mean that you're blotting the family record, Pete."

"I know you didn't," Pete said, "but I'm not exactly enhancing it. . . . So I kept thinking, why do Mom and Dad have to know? I managed to grow up without opening that boil. Why start all the guilt/blame machinery going now? I was never crazy about self-revelation, either. I always hated people who got on the tube and confessed they were alcoholics or anorexics or Jesus freaks or some other damn thing!"

I said, "When I'd watch gays on talk shows, I'd wonder why they'd announce it. Dad said they were exhibitionists."

"I thought they were, too," Pete said. "I used to sit

watching those things hoping to God they'd look as straight as possible. I used to hate seeing any Charlie Gilhooleys coming out of the closet."

"Poor Charlie just got beat up at the Kingdom By The Sea bar," I said.

"I'm sorry, but I'm not surprised," Pete said. "I used to stay as far away from Charlie Gilhooley as possible. Sometimes, when I was a kid, *I* felt like beating him up. I'd tell myself I might be gay, but I'm not a Charlie Gilhooley fairy!"

"Well, you're not," I said.

"So what?" said Pete. "Do I get extra points for not looking it? . . . I used to think I did."

"Then what changed you?" I said. "What made you tell Mom?"

Pete took a fast gulp of coffee, and it sloshed down the side of his mug to the tabletop. "Jim Stanley went to work on me," he said.

He started to get up, for something to wipe up the coffee.

"I'll get it," I said.

I went into the kitchen for a sponge. I was trying to remember Jim Stanley. I'd met him only once. He wrote science-fiction stories and screenplays as J. J. Stanley, and called himself "bicoastal" because he traveled back and forth from New York to Beverly Hills. Pete had gone to Europe with him last summer.

When they came back, we'd all had dinner together, at a restaurant in SoHo, in lower New York. Pete and Jim had just come from having drinks at Stan and Tina Horton's loft down there. Jim was Pete's age, tall, sandy-haired. I remembered he'd talked a lot about Rachter, this program that rigged a computer to write novels. He was working on an idea for a TV series about a Rachterlike character in an office, who told stories about the employees. . . . I couldn't remember anything else about him.

While I wiped up the coffee, Pete said, "Jim's a political gay. I used to hate gay activists! I used to think they were a bunch of self-pitying sissies who blamed everything on the fact they were homosexuals. I used to tell Jim that what I did in bed was my own private business. Jim said that was right: What I did in bed *was*, but what about life out of bed? What about lying to everyone, trying to pass for straight, never letting family or friends know what was going on in my life? . . . He convinced me the only way to get past that kind of self-hatred was to come out of hiding. He said anyone who loved me wouldn't love me any less if I came out, and I'd like myself a lot more. So I started with Mom. You were next on my list."

I tossed the sponge at the sink, missed, left it on the kitchen floor. "What'd Mom say when you told her?"

"She said she wasn't surprised. She said she was glad I told her. And she said she used to worry that I was too much of a loner."

"That's what I always thought you were, too," I said. "A loner." I sat down.

"I was. A busy loner."

"What's a busy loner?"

"Active, but not really attached," Pete said. "Too busy. . . . That's why I never did anything about finishing *The Skids*—or finishing my Ph.D."

"Oh, *that*," I said a little contemptuously, as though Dad was in the room with us.

"Dad was right about that," Pete said. "I should have gone to Columbia, or N.Y.U., and finished it. I should have worked on my book, too," Pete said. "But when I landed here right out of Princeton, I couldn't believe the gay scene. It was still the seventies. There'll never be another time like it. I thought I'd died and gone to heaven. I wasn't out at Princeton, naturally. When I saw all the gay bars and discos here, I just wanted to dance and drink and play."

I couldn't imagine Pete dancing with another guy.

I said, "When I get out of college, if I ever get into college, I'll probably want to dance and drink and play, too."

Pete shook his head. "No. You're having your party right now. My adolescence was on hold. . . . I could hardly take Tim Lathrop to the Seaville High Prom, or Marty to the P-Party. We sneaked around like guilty thieves. Tim spent half his time at confession, and Marty was seeing if a shrink could make him straight. . . . That's when I became the world's foremost authority on gay books." Pete laughed. "Migod! I don't think there's a book that even remotely touched on the subject that I didn't read. I spent hours in the library looking under H in the card catalog!"

I was remembering Tim Lathrop as Pete talked. Tim had been a lifeguard on Main Beach when Pete was. He was this blond hunk who was at our house a lot when Pete was in his teens, one of the star tennis players at Holy Family High. . . . Marty Olivetti was still one of Pete's closest friends. He was from Tulsa, Oklahoma. He'd come from Princeton with Pete for weekends years ago, and they'd spent most of their time out on the boat. When Dad first met him, I remembered Dad'd imitate Marty's thick Oklahoma accent, and tease, "What kind of an Italian says 'far' for 'fire' and 'pank' for 'pink'?"

Pete got up to get himself another cup of coffee. A minute later he zapped me with the soggy sponge I'd left on the kitchen floor, calling me *"Cochon!"*

I threw it back at him, and for a while we were feinting punches at each other, and ducking, horsing around in the old familiar way.

But Pete looked beat. When I said I ought to be leaving soon, Pete didn't protest. He said he probably shouldn't have any more coffee—it'd only give him the trots.

Pete said he needed a nap, too, that Stan and Tina were coming by later, and Jim was flying in from the coast that night. He said he'd try to bring Jim out to Seaville for dinner one night next week.

"Does Jim know you have this thing?" I asked him.

"Say AIDS, Ricky," Pete said. "Mom and Dad are calling it a thing, a bug, everything but AIDS. . . . Yes, Jim knows. We were both sick all through Europe. I kept telling myself I had what he had, some kind of dysentery. But my lymph nodes were swollen, and I had these little red spots on my ankles. I had all these explanations to myself for what they were. But I couldn't ever get my strength back, and there were more spots. I began to really panic by the time I came out to Seaville last time. Mom wanted me to go see Doctor Rapp there. By then I had this big purple bruise under my arm. When I saw that, I began to face the fact I could have AIDS. I figured old Rapp would broadcast it all over The Hadefield Club. Dad would like that a lot!"

"Stop worrying about Dad," I said, as Pete helped me get on my blazer.

"I worry about him the most," Pete said. "I think

this is going to be hardest on Dad. Most of the time he spent here last night, he was on the phone to Phil Kerin. Do you remember Doctor Kerin? One of Dad's old golf cronies?"

"Dad told me he called him."

"Dad must have said 'This is confidential' a dozen times during the conversation. . . . I could have gone from the hospital to Dad's place last night, but Dad was afraid to let you kids stay here. He said if it ever got out that I have AIDS, and he'd known you kids were here, he'd be responsible for putting you at risk."

"I don't get that," I said. "Dad told me there was no way you could catch it casually."

"He's worried that other people don't know that."

"Dad makes everything hard!"

"No, Ricky. This time it's just hard. It's not Dad."

We stood there facing each other a minute.

I said, "I just want you to get well."

"You've made me feel better, pal. Thanks," Pete said. He slung his arm around my shoulder. "The last thing Dad said to me last night was 'Whoever got the bright idea to come up with the name 'gay'?" Pete was doing a good imitation of Dad at his darkest. " 'It doesn't sound like a very *gay* life to me!' "

Pete began walking me down the hall. "I told him it has its moments. . . . Who was it that said moments are all anyone gets, anyway? Thoreau? Or was it

Oscar Wilde? . . . Speaking of Oscar, Ricky, Dad keeps reminding me something has to be done for Oscar."

We stood by the door talking about me taking Oscar to the vet. Pete said we should get the vet's opinion first. If the vet thought it was time, Pete would come out and hold Oscar while he got the injection.

While we discussed it, I remembered in English class, in eighth grade once, we'd read "The Ballad of Reading Gaol" by Oscar Wilde. During the discussion afterward, Roman Knight got everyone in the back of the classroom laughing, and Miss Rix said, "If you have anything to add to this discussion, Roman, stand up and tell the whole class."

Roman got up, performed a curtsy, and said in this high falsetto: "Geth why Othger Wilde went to pri-thin?"

Right before I opened Pete's door, I said, "Oscar isn't named after Oscar *Wilde*, is he?"

"That's who he's named after," Pete said.

"You named him that when you were thirteen?"

"Yeah, and you were what? Three? Four?" Pete leaned against the wall. "I was always precocious, Ricky."

"You were also probably the only one in the family who ever knew Oscar's last name," I said.

"Or that he even had one," said Pete.

Ten

THE NEXT SATURDAY, right after Seaville's game with Greenport, Dill was driving to Massachusetts with her family to see the Wheaton campus.

"That's like Dill, to wait until *after* the game," Jack said. "Dill loves being a pom-pom girl. She's easy—not like Nicki. Nicki probably won't even show up to see me play."

We were heading toward school early, so Jack could suit up. I always drove Jack to games in his Mustang. He claimed he got too nervous to concentrate on the road.

"Nicki's changed since we went to New York," Jack said.

I let him talk. All week I'd gone out of my way to avoid Nicki.

"She's got something on her mind," Jack said.

"Maybe she's worried about all the trouble Toledo started," I said. Charlie Gilhooley'd refused to press charges, but a gay organization had championed his cause, and the local paper'd joined in and said Kingdom By The Sea should clean up its act, not only in their attitude toward customers they refused service, but in their tawdry, honky-tonk ambiance and appearance.

"It's not that," Jack said. "She's cooling off with me."

I'd seen Charlie Gilhooley walking around with both arms in slings. I could go a year without ever noticing Charlie, but that week it seemed like I saw him mincing past me every time I turned a corner. . . . I heard differently that week, too. Once I whirled around in the kitchen, where Mrs. Tompkins was listening to the radio while she was getting dinner. I could have sworn the announcer said that homosexuals were at half price.

"What's at half price? What'd that guy just say?"

Mrs. Tompkins said, "Diamond's is having their fall sale on home essentials. Everything's half price."

Jack was chewing on a Milky Way. "Sometimes I think Dill makes Nicki feel inferior. Dill. Jeannie Gaelen—those girls get to her. She claims she couldn't care less about them, but they're all she talks about. She knows Dill hates her."

"Dill doesn't hate her. She doesn't know how to relate to her."

"We shouldn't have gone on that weekend. That did it."

"You didn't do it? The weekend did it?"

"I shouldn't have passed out on the rug. Did I snore?"

"You snored. Your fly was open."

"Sure, and I suppose I farted, too."

"What do you want to hear? That you were beautiful? Why don't you just stop drinking around her?"

"Why don't you stop growing chin pimples? . . . You don't even listen to what I'm telling you anymore. I'm changing. I want to be somebody now."

"Maybe you could be a cartoon character in one of America's theme parks."

"That's what I mean. You've got a million zingers, but not one word of advice."

"Jack," I said, "what in hell am I supposed to say?"

"Help me figure this girl out! You've been around more than I have. You just keep saying not to pounce. I know damn well she was probably in the sack with Ski on the first date!"

"Forget about Ski. Don't try to compete with Ski. But let her talk about him if she wants to. . . . Talk with her, Jack."

"About *what*?"

"About anything she wants to talk about."

"Yeah. I'm not a big talker, but she's one."

"You're not going to be able to compete with Ski, so go the other way. Pretend you're fascinated by her mind."

"I sort of am."

"Good. Then you don't have to pretend."

"But I'm more fascinated by her body. I get so hot around her, it's embarrassing."

"Try to forget her body for tonight."

"How do I do that?"

Good question. "Just do it," I said. "Just tell yourself you're not going to treat her like riffraff. She claims you're the first one who didn't treat her like riffraff. Be affectionate. With *words*, not your hands."

"I told her I love her."

"You said I love you?"

"Yeah."

"I love you? I. Love. You?"

"I. Love. You. Yeah."

"Well, good. Good."

"What'll we do after the movie?"

"Take her to Sweet Mouth."

"Not to Montauk Point?"

"Not tonight."

"Maybe I'm scared shitless to have sex with her! Maybe I should get some experience first."

"Where are you going to get experience? What is she supposed to do while you're getting experience?"

"I'm just going to take her out to Montauk Point after the movie," Jack said. "I'll talk with her out there."

"You'll screw it up out there is what you'll do."

"I'm not going to listen to you," Jack said. "It's like the blind leading the blind!"

"Do what you want to do!" I snapped at him. "I've got my own problems!"

"I know you have," Jack said.

"What do you mean you know I have?"

"I know what's bugging you, buddy. Don't you think I know you by now?"

I waited.

"Dill's going to get into Wheaton," Jack said, "and where does that leave you? Right?"

He got out near the gym. I drove the Mustang down to the parking lot behind school.

I turned off the motor, turned the key back in the ignition, and sat there listening to the radio for a while. I listened to songs by Glenn Frey, Wham!, DeBarge, and Survivor. They were all about love: losing it, getting it, wanting it, leaving it.

I finally got out. I started walking toward the stadium.

It was real football weather: blue skies and sun, but cold.

People were trooping along in coats and scarves, and the wind was shaking what autumn leaves were left off the trees.

I saw her right away.

I think she saw me see her. She was with Cap. He had on sunglasses and that hat he always wore tilted over his eyes, his arm around some girl who didn't look much older than Nicki.

I changed direction.

I headed down the bleachers toward the field, where the pom-pom girls were warming up in their maroon skirts and white sweaters.

Dill ran toward me, hugging herself against the cold. She wanted to know what the doctor said about Oscar. She knew I'd taken him to the vet's that morning.

"It's definitely time," I told Dill. I'd told Pete the same thing on the telephone. Pete said he'd try to get out next week. He said there were a lot of things keeping him in New York, and that Jim was having daily meetings at NBC about the new series he was writing.

Dill said all the things you say, what a long happy life Oscar'd had and how lucky we were we could help pets out of their misery, that it was too bad human beings couldn't do the same for people they loved. I said yes, right, I know it, and Dill asked me if I was okay.

"Fine!"

"I have to get back!" Dill said. "We're working on our new jump-and-turn cheer. . . . What are you going to do tonight?"

"Think of you," automatically.

"Besides that?"

"No plans." Mom and Dad were both driving back from New York sometime that night. Mom in her car,

Dad in his. Mom had driven in Thursday night to have dinner with Pete and Jim Stanley. The one thing we hadn't done all week was talk about it. If I wasn't working, Mom was at play rehearsals. Evenings at dinner, Mrs. Tompkins was right nearby in the kitchen.

Dill said, "We're leaving right after the game, so I want a kiss now. You know Daddy. He'd hate it if he had to wait while I tried to find you after the game."

While I was kissing her, the Greenport High School band came marching out on the field playing "Alouette."

I could see myself when I was a little kid, patting myself on the head while Pete sang *"Je te plumerai la tête, Et la tête, et la tête"*; then we'd both chorus *"Alouette! Alouette!"*

"I'll be in some tacky New England motel watching *Saturday Night Live* tonight, thinking of you watching it, too," Dill said. "You're going to watch it, aren't you?"

I did an imitation of Martin Short playing Ed Grimley, with his pomaded hair coming to a point on the top of his head. I did his little kooky skip and said what he'd have said, "It's an awfully decent show, I must say."

The team came running out on the field. The pompom girls began shouting, *"Kick 'em in the shins! Kick 'em in the knees! We get higher S.A.T.s!"*

I went up in the bleachers and talked with Dill's folks for a while. Dill's father asked me how my college plans were coming. I never talked with him when he didn't ask me that. I said things were in the works, and he had that same slanted smile Dill had as he said you're always saying that, *what* things are in the works?

"Don't interrogate him, Bertie!" Dill's mother said. I thought of the sampler his sister had on her wall, with the words "Give fate a good fight, anyway."

"I'm not interrogating him," Mr. Dilberto said. "I'm asking him what things are in the works?"

"I'm trying to decide between Harvard and Yale," I said.

Mr. Dilberto said, "You're a real wiseass, aren't you?"

I moved around, sat some, stood some, and halfway through the game, she came down to where I was standing.

She actually had on pants. I don't think I'd ever seen her in pants. They were blue cargo-pocket pants she wore with a man-tailored jacket several sizes too large for her, a white sweater under it, a white silk scarf around her neck, and the black-leather fedora tipped over her green eyes. She had on high heels. Her blond hair was spilling past her shoulders. She kept pushing it back from her eyes with her long, thin fingers while she spoke to me.

"How are things with you?" she said.

"How are things with you?"

"I asked you first. I get the feeling you're ignoring me."

"Jack's not playing very well today."

"I'm not talking about Jack."

"What are you talking about?" I felt cruel. I knew what she was talking about.

"Are you mad at me, Erick?"

"Un-uh."

"You act like you are."

"I'm not."

"I never come to these things."

"Well, you wanted to see Jack play."

"I didn't come because of Jack. . . . You act like you're mad."

"I'm Jack's best friend," I said. "That's how I'm trying to act."

"But what about how *you* feel?"

"You're Jack's girlfriend."

"Because he says so?"

"That's good enough for me," I said.

We just stood there. I was thinking that someday I'd find out the name of that perfume.

Behind us Roman Knight began singing his own version of Billy Squier's "Eye on You."

He was singing it at Nicki: Got my eye on you, tossing her name into the verse.

"What does he want with you?" I asked her.

"Ask him."

"He always seems to start in when you show up."

"He's probably bored out of his gourd with Jeannie Gaelen. . . . I'm not talking about Roman Knight now."

"What perfume do you wear?"

"It's called First."

"First at what?"

"It's just called First. First in the hearts of your countrymen. First at bat. First in line. I don't know why it's called First. See, I didn't name it. . . . First in your heart?"

"Nicki, I've got to go."

"It's only halftime."

"I've got an appointment. I'm already late for this appointment."

"Here's something for you," she said. She reached into her jacket pocket and handed me a piece of folded paper.

"What's that?"

"You won't know until you look at it," she said, "but don't look at it now."

I said I'd see her, and I gave her a little two-fingered salute and started walking. I kept going. I guessed I was going home. I knew that when I got there, the house would be empty. I'd start thinking about Pete again.

But I went anyway.

I waited until I was all the way up in the parking lot to unfold the slip of paper Nicki'd passed to me.

It said: *Don't say you don't feel it, too, because I won't believe you.*

Eleven

EARLY SATURDAY NIGHT I scraped and coated the kitchen chairs Mom had been after me to paint for so long.

Then I made a fire, turned on TV, and took the meat loaf Mrs. Tompkins had left for me into the living room with a can of Dr Pepper.

I watched Richard Gere make love to Debra Winger in *An Officer and a Gentleman*, thinking Dill'd look a little like Debra Winger if she'd let her hair grow. That movie was one of those I'd just as soon not have watched with Dill. She'd have liked it a lot, but I'd have ended up feeling the way I always did when I saw something like that with her: like some skinny kid still putting Clearasil on his zits and scheming with other nerds how to get it on with a girl.

Maybe Dill and I knew each other too well, I was thinking, and I was also thinking of Nicki, all through the movie. I'd put the note from her into my strongbox, in the bottom drawer of my desk. There was a letter in there from Pete, too, written to me the spring I'd become thirteen. It was on Princeton stationery. It began, "Welcome to your teens, pal. *Prendre la lune avec les dents!*"

I remember when I translated it, I couldn't figure out what Pete was trying to tell me. Seize the moon with my teeth? Pete had to tell me later that it meant aim at impossibilities.

While I watched *Saturday Night Live*, I began reviewing ratio and proportions for the S.A.T.s coming up in a month. I was figuring out how many minutes it would take a train traveling at the rate of 45 miles per hour to cover a distance of 4/5 of a mile, when I heard Mom come through the back door.

I hollered out, "Don't sit on the kitchen chairs!"

"Oh, you did them! What a nice surprise!" She came into the living room in her belted polo coat, complaining about an accident on the Montauk Highway that had stopped traffic. "Your father was going to leave about an hour after I did. He was having dinner near Sloan-Kettering hospital with Phil Kerin, so I don't know when he'll get here."

The Kinks were guesting on *Saturday Night Live*, and I noticed her flinch at the sound. I turned it down and helped her out of her coat.

"Erick, your father has his heart set on us all going

to church together tomorrow, so don't give him a hard time about it, honey. Okay?"

"Okay," I agreed. "How's Pete?"

"It isn't good," she said. "Your father wants us to wait, and all talk about it together tomorrow."

"What about Jim?"

"What about him?"

"What do you think of him?"

"He's very supportive of Pete, and Pete needs that now."

"Do you like him?"

"I like him."

Mom looked tired. She came across to me and mussed up my hair in an affectionate gesture. "Are you okay, dear?"

"Why wouldn't I be okay?"

"You're taking this thing better than Dad or me, I think. I don't mean just Pete's illness. I mean finding out about Pete so suddenly, and not having time to deal with it before you deal with the illness. It just all came rushing at you."

It was the first time we'd really had a chance to talk about it.

"I don't have any problem with Pete being homosexual," I said. "Do you?"

"Of course I have a problem with it!"

"Pete didn't seem to think so."

"My problem with it isn't a priority right now."

"Pete said you told him you weren't surprised."

"I wasn't *surprised*. I was in total shock when he told me."

"What about telling Pete you were glad he wasn't a loner?"

"What about it?" Mom said. "Pete was leaving for Europe when he sprang it on me. What was I supposed to say? I didn't want him to go away feeling he'd pulled the rug out from under me. I didn't want him worrying all summer about how I'd reacted."

"We shouldn't have a problem with his being gay, Mom."

"Shouldn't we? I think we should. Don't be too sure you're not having any problem with it, either. There's a delayed reaction. There certainly was for me," Mom said. "But Pete's too ill for any of that. . . . Do you know that Jim wants Pete to go to the coast with him?"

"Are they supposed to be going together or something?"

"I was going to ask you that very question. I don't know. I suppose they are. I think Jim's very taken with Pete. How do I know what Pete feels? Obviously, I never knew."

She took something out of her bag and handed it to me. "Jim gave me this. He said we should all read it carefully."

It was a pamphlet called "About AIDS." It was issued by Gay Inquiry.

"I'm going to leave it up in your room, honey, after I look at it. I don't want it lying around where Mrs. Tompkins can see it. All right?"

"All right." I handed it back to her. "You look beat, Mom. Get some rest."

"I'm going to," she said. "Tomorrow, after church, Dad and you and I will have a long talk."

I turned up the TV and tried to concentrate on a problem about a motorist on the freeway, covering 0.8 miles in a minute, when I heard Jack come in the back door, calling my name.

"Hey, you're early," I said.

"I feel like getting smashed!"

"What happened?"

"Christ if I know! I could use a drink!"

"There's beer out in the refrigerator."

Jack sat down beside me. "Everything just fell apart in Sweet Mouth. That was my mistake, taking her there."

"What fell apart?"

"Everything! She can't take the crowd! I've been pushing her into things. Not sex. I'm not talking about sex."

"Start from the beginning."

"We went to see the movie with Madonna in it. She

really liked it. My mistake was taking her to Sweet Mouth after. Before that, my mistake was pushing her into trying out for pom-pom."

"Stop talking about your mistakes."

"Your mistake. Sweet Mouth was your idea," Jack said.

"Don't blame it on me. What happened?"

"Everybody was in Sweet Mouth tonight. Roman Knight sat right behind us with Jeannie Gaelen."

"And he started making cracks."

"How'd you know?"

"He always does."

"I was ready to belt him one, but Nicki said just ignore him. He was going Hel-*lo*, Nick-ki! That's all, but it got to her. She started talking about how it was my crowd but it wasn't her crowd. She said she didn't have a crowd, and she didn't want a crowd."

"*And?*"

"I said it wasn't my crowd, either. I said I didn't care about them, either, but she said I was into the whole bit: double-dating, football, dragging her home to meet my folks. She said *dragging* like I'd forced her there kicking and screaming, so I got mad and said she ought to be honored that I'd invited her to my house."

"Honored? Jesus!"

"That just came out, and I tried to take it back, but

she said oh, honored, honored; oh, I didn't know it was such an honor. Like that."

"Go on."

"Then she just looks at me across the table and says it's all over."

"*All* over?" I said, as though there was over and *all* over.

"All over," Jack said. "She said she was going to tell me anyway, even before we got in there she'd planned to tell me she didn't want to date me anymore."

He punched his palm with his fist and got up. "I'll take that beer now."

"I'm sorry, Jack."

"*You're* sorry? I'm wiped out! You want a beer? Have a beer."

"I can't. . . . You can get me another Dr Pepper."

I went across and turned down the TV. I figured we were in for a long night of talking. I closed a Barron's S.A.T. review course and put it on the coffee table. Then I checked to be sure Oscar was okay in his bed, behind the couch.

I was thinking that I had to tell Jack. Listen to him first. Then tell him something had started up between Nicki and me—by accident. Tell him it was no big deal, just this little sideline shit going down. This accident.

He could blow. He could tell me to go screw myself,

and that the whole thing sucked, but we'd get past it. That would be the end of it then.

When Jack didn't come back with the drinks, I went into the kitchen. Jack was sitting in one of the newly painted chairs at the kitchen table, holding his head with his hands.

"I'm really wiped out!" he said.

"You're also sitting in fresh paint. I tipped the chairs forward, hoping no one'd sit down."

"My God, I just paid sixty dollars for these jeans and a hundred and sixty for the jacket!"

"Then get them off, fast. Let them dry. You can't do anything about them until they dry."

"This isn't my night, Erick."

He got his Guess? jeans and jacket off, and I got him a beer, got myself a Dr Pepper.

We went back into the living room and sat on the couch while Jack said, "I read her all wrong, that's all. All I was thinking about was sex, and all she was thinking about was *them*. That's what she calls everybody: them. That New York weekend was a lousy idea!"

"It was *her* idea!"

"She just wanted to see Bruce Springsteen."

"She didn't ask me to get tickets for you and her. She wanted us all to go."

"She thought that was the only way she could get to see him. . . . I never should have dragged her home to meet my folks. She calls that family-around-the-table crap!"

"The hell with what she calls it! She should have said she didn't want to go home and meet your folks!"

"She did say it! I wouldn't listen! I never let her talk. . . . I practically forced her to try out for pom-pom. I *did* force her!"

"Don't be so down on yourself. This girl isn't worth it!"

"What the hell do you know?" Jack said. "I'm in love with Nicki!"

I thought he was going to break down and cry.

I scooted down closer to him and put my hand on his wrist.

I said, "Jack, listen. You're my best friend."

"I know. I don't know what I'd do without you."

That stopped me for a second. I wanted to think how to put it.

"You should have seen her face," Jack said.

I could see her face. I could see the cigarette in her mouth, the smoke curling up, that one eyebrow cocked, the green of her eyes.

Jack said, "She looked straight at me and said, 'It's all over, Jack.' "

He was shaking. He had trouble getting words out. He said, "I just meet someone I really love and she tells me it's all over."

"Jack," I said, but he wouldn't let me go on.

He said, "I never . . . ever . . . felt this way about anyone!"

I put my arm around him.

That was the scene Dad walked in on: Jack in his shorts on the couch saying he'd never ever felt that way about anyone, me with my arm around him.

Dad barked, "What the hell is going on!"

I began, "Jack's had some—"

I was going to say "some bad news," but Dad didn't let me finish.

"Beer!" Dad finished it. Dad's eyes were blazing.

"Erick's not drinking, though, Mr. Rudd." Jack thought Dad was mad about that. The bottle of Molson's ale was right in front of me.

Dad had murder in his eyes. He began marching, that was the only way to describe it. He marched across the room to the stairway. Then he marched up the stairs.

"Now *he's* pissed off at me," Jack said, "for drinking his Molson's."

It'd never occur to Jack what Dad was really angry at.

Upstairs a door slammed so hard it shook the house.

Even old, deaf Oscar jumped.

That ended our conversation.

Twelve

"HONEY?" Mom was at my bedroom door. "You'd better get up right now, if you're going to go to church with us."

"I'm not."

I was lying on my side, under the covers. I could hear Mom come all the way into the room.

"Remember last night I asked you not to give Dad a hard time about church this morning?"

"Dad can go to hell," I mumbled.

I could hear a hard rain on the roof.

"Dad made a mistake," Mom said. "He was exhausted by the time he got here last night."

"Some mistake."

As soon as Jack's car had left, Mom had come downstairs. I don't know what Dad'd told her, but her face was white as milk. I said go in the kitchen and look at the chair Jack sat in. I said he took off his pants and coat to let the paint dry, so you'd better rush back upstairs and tell Dad not to worry, he has only one fag son, not two. Mom said she'd slap my face if she ever heard me say that word again.

Before I'd gone to sleep, I'd tossed the pamphlet about AIDS on the floor, beside my socks and Nikes. Mom went around to the side of my bed and picked it up. "Erick, I told you I don't want this lying around where Mrs. Tompkins can see it." She stuck it in my bureau drawer.

"What are we going to tell Mrs. Tompkins and everyone else, that Pete is dying of a bug he picked up in Paris?"

Mom whirled around. "What did you just say?"

"That pamphlet says it's always fatal."

"I don't care what it says. That's not necessarily true."

"Didn't you read it?"

"Just get up, Erick. We're going to talk about it later."

"I'm not going to church with Dad."

"He's counting on it."

"Tough! I was counting on him to know me a little better than he seems to. I was counting on him to know Jack a little better, too."

"Don't start all this now," Mom said. "I don't have the patience."

She went out of the room and slammed the door.

I listened to the rain for a while. Then I heard him coming down the hall, his footsteps mad. Oh, *he's* mad, I thought. Beautiful.

Then he was in my room.

"I overreacted last night, Erick. I was tired. I'd had a long session with Phil Kerin, and there was a traffic tie-up on the Montauk Highway."

"I can't believe you thought what you thought."

"I can't believe you got around to painting those chairs."

"And never mind *me*. You've known Jack since he was born."

"I've known Pete since he was born, too."

"I'm not Pete! Neither is Jack."

"I said I was sorry."

"No, you didn't. You said you'd overreacted."

"All right. I'm sorry."

"I'm not going to forget that one."

"Then forgive it. That's what church is for, anyway: forgiveness. Get out of bed and get dressed!"

"I'm not ready to forgive it, either."

"What do you care what I thought? Last weekend you said it was just another way of being."

"It's not what I choose for myself, that's all."

"Pete tells me it's not a matter of choice."

"I don't know what the hell it is! I only know I'm not that way!"

"Then you have something to be thankful for! Church is for that, too. Get up! Now!"

I knew he'd wait until I slung my legs over the side of the bed. "Mom gave me a booklet that says AIDS is always fatal," I said. "How come that's never been mentioned?"

"We're going to talk after church," Dad said. "First we'll pray."

I was almost dressed when Jack called.

"I'm rushing now, Jack. I have to go to church with the family."

"Could you talk to Nicki, Erick? She respects your opinions. Tell her I'm going crazy. Tell her just to see me. She won't see me."

"She's not worth all this, Jack."

"Would I tell you Dill wasn't worth it if you were going through something with Dill?"

"She's not Dill."

"Just talk to her. Please?"

"I don't know when I can do that. After church we're having dinner at The Frog Pond."

"Tell your dad I'm getting him a six-pack of Molson's."

"He's not mad about that," I said. "He was mad about a traffic tie-up on the Montauk Highway."

"Will you go to see Nicki for me?"

"Not today. I can't. . . . You don't know her, Jack. She's not worth this."

"Oh, *you* know her, huh?" Jack said.

"I know she's not worth all this shit."

"You said you liked her fine."

"I lied." I was trying to sound as though I was joking with him, but my tone sounded more bitter than funny, because if it hadn't been for Jack I'd probably have thought she was worth any kind of shit I had to take.

"Thanks for nothing again, Erick," and Jack hung up.

Reverend Shorr had been the pastor of St. Luke's for as long as I could remember, going way back to when Pete was in his teens. Shorr was a thin little fellow with gold-rimmed glasses who always read his sermons and made them sound like instructions for assembling mail-order items. He was known as Reverend Snore by some of his parishioners. He wasn't hail-fellow-well-met enough for a lot of them. He was too humorless and pedantic, and old-timers said he didn't "look" like St. Luke's.

Some years back Dad was on a secret committee bent on replacing Shorr with someone who had more charisma.

Pete kept saying it just wasn't like Dad to concern himself with something so parochial. Pete kept nag-

ging at Dad to find out the real reason Dad wanted
Shorr out. (Pete always stuck up for losers; he had kind
of an amused affection for old Snore, too).

Then Pete found out what was behind Dad's rancor.
It seemed Reverend Shorr had resigned from The
Hadefield Club, known by some locals as The Hate-
Filled Club, because the club discriminated against
nearly everyone but rich WASPS, and wouldn't even
let Jews make visits there with members.

Dad was an old Hadefield man who'd been spon-
sored for membership by Mom's family. Dad played
golf there, swam off its beaches in summer, and wined
and dined clients in the dining room. Although Mom
eventually refused to swim or play tennis there, she
still went to the club when Dad wanted to go. It was
about the only place in Seaville where Dad ever did
want to go.

Dad claimed Shorr had gone out of his way to make
an issue of certain "traditions" the club had.

"Like the tradition of being rich, and privileged,
and prejudiced?" Pete would ask Dad.

"There's nothing wrong with being rich and privileged and selective," Dad would answer.

"Prejudiced!" Pete would insist.

"Selective!" Dad would shoot back at him. "It's a
private club."

I was around six or seven when these arguments

between Dad and Pete were going on. They lasted through a whole long, hot summer. You could hear their shouts almost any night along the street we lived on. Jack and I would sit out on the curb, pretending to plug our ears with our fingers, me always marveling at Pete for taking Dad on that way. I wasn't that kind of a fighter. Even if I had been a fighter, Dad would have been at the bottom of any list of potential opponents I'd put together.

Finally, at the end of that summer, on Dad's birthday, Pete gave Dad a present that made Dad so angry, he actually took a swing at Pete. Dad never resorted to violence. He'd never hit Pete or me when we were growing up. But when he took this T-shirt out of the wrapping paper, held it up, and read it, he went for Pete.

The front of the T-shirt read:

THE HADEFIELD CLUB

and on the back it said:

WHOEVER HAS THE MOST THINGS
WHEN HE DIES, WINS.

"One great advantage to being subjected to one of old Snore's sermons," said Dad after church that morning, "is that he never captures your attention. I appreciated that this morning. I needed time to think."

"I like Reverend Shorr," said Mom. "He's old-fashioned and he's familiar."

We were driving down Woody Path toward the ocean. We often went there after church. When it was raining, as it was that morning, we stayed in the car and watched the ocean.

"I can't believe you don't want to eat at The Club," Mom said as we passed the Hadefield drive and went toward the public beach. "The Frog Pond isn't known for very substantial food. Chicken. Fish."

"That's exactly what Phil told me I should start eating, last night at dinner," Dad said. "Chicken. Fish. Cut back on the red meat, eat more salads and vegetables. . . . And we'll have more privacy at The Frog Pond."

That was the *real* reason, I figured. Dad was making sure we wouldn't bring up anything about Pete around club members.

"I've been telling you to cut back on red meat for years," Mom said.

"You're not an oncologist," Dad said.

"What's an oncologist?" I asked him.

"A cancer specialist. One of the manifestations of Pete's AIDS is a rare form of cancer. It's called Kaposi's sarcoma. It's a tumor of the blood vessels," Dad said.

I remembered reading that in the pamphlet Mom had lent me, but most of what I'd read hadn't really made a dent yet. I kept telling myself it didn't pertain to Pete.

We drove to where we had a view of the ocean, parked, and had coffee from the thermos Mrs. Tompkins always put in the car.

We usually saved anything serious to talk about until after church, when we came here. Usually it was my stuff we got into: the S.A.T.s, college, things that were going down in my life that Dad had missed because he was in New York all week.

That morning Dad talked about Pete.

Dad said what Pete had *was* fatal, but every day there was new headway being made, and ongoing research. We had to think positively, Dad said. There were still plenty of AIDS victims who hadn't died yet.

"Plenty?" Mom said.

"Some," Dad said. "Enough."

Pete had decided to resign from Southworth School. Jim Stanley had persuaded Pete to accompany him to San Francisco, to see a doctor there.

"And after that fool's errand," said Dad, "Pete will come home to us."

"Pete told me he was going to Beverly Hills with Jim after San Francisco," Mom said.

"Pete will come home!" Dad insisted. "We're his family! What the hell is Jim Stanley to Pete? He spouts off this gay rhetoric that even embarrasses Pete!"

"I think Jim has good intentions," Mom said.

Dad snapped, "And the road to hell is paved with good intentions! I know the top oncologist in the country, and Pete trusts some science fiction writer, and something that calls itself Gay Inquiry!"

Dad glowered down at his coffee. "Gay Inquiry! Who the hell with cancer is going to trust someplace that calls itself *gay* anything? Does homosexuality affect the brain?"

Mom said, "Gay Inquiry has been investigating AIDS for a longer time than anyplace else. They've put their stamp of approval on the research this San Francisco doctor's done."

"Oh, their stamp of approval?" Dad thundered. "Is it a gay stamp? Is their stamp of approval one of those yellow-and-black happy faces?"

"What will it hurt if Pete sees this doctor?" Mom said.

"Why should Pete settle for second best, when Phil Kerin's the best there is? Just because someplace with gay in front of its name recommends it!"

"I thought we were going to talk about this calmly, Arthur."

"We *are*," Dad said.

"When do we begin?" I said.

"Right now," he said. He set the plastic cup of coffee

on the dashboard and took out a paper napkin to wipe his mouth.

The waves were really high. I thought of summer mornings early, before the sun had risen all the way up—I'd come down here with Pete and watch him dive into the waves on his surfboard.

Those summers he worked as a lifeguard on Main Beach, we'd get here before he was on duty. He'd try to get me interested in surfing, but I was more the sand castle type.

Mom'd be afraid he'd break his neck. She'd remind him that Michelle had never been a reckless girl, but look what had happened to Michelle. Pete would have to listen to that while he was making his sandwiches for lunch. He'd say Mom, Mom, I'll be careful. When I see that big wave, *Je plongerai!* Mom would laugh back at him, and they'd jabber away in French. Pete always knew how to relax her. He could always get around her, get her smiling again.

"First of all," Dad began, "I apologize for losing my cool, as Erick might say."

"As anyone might say," I said.

I was in the backseat of the Chrysler, sitting forward, resting my elbows on the front seat. Mom reached up and put her hand on my wrist, as though to warn me not to go too far, let Dad play this his way.

Dad said, "I don't like what Pete is, and I don't like

what Pete has, but none of that matters now! I'm going to try and keep my feelings out of this conversation."

"Good!" Mom agreed. "Let's just talk about what we're going to do."

"And what we're *not* going to do," said Dad. "We're not going to take anyone into our confidence. Not anyone!"

Mom said, "I've been telling people that Pete has a virus, and he does have a virus."

"There is no point in *offering any* information about Pete's health!" Dad said.

"Arthur? I think we have to tell Mrs. Tompkins. She lives with us. She's like family."

"She's *not* family, though. Another person's secret is like another person's money: You're not so careful with it as you are of your own."

"I think we're morally obligated to let her know, or let her go," Mom said. "Pete will be coming out to the house. She has a right to make up her own mind about whether or not she thinks she's at risk."

"She's not at risk, Laura."

"I said whether or not she *thinks* she's at risk."

"If she's not at risk, what sense is there in giving her a chance to decide whether or not she *thinks* she's at risk?"

"What about Jack?" I said. "He's around a lot too."

"A lot is right!" Dad barked. "In his jockeys, drinking my beer! Okay, he had paint on his pants, but you were sitting there with your arm around him!"

"Arthur!"

"He had his arm around Jack!"

"I'm not even going to listen to this!" I said.

But I listened.

Dad said, "I'm not accusing anyone of anything! But maybe if we'd paid a little more attention to what Pete was doing when he was Erick's age, we wouldn't be in this situation!"

Mom said, "Now listen to me. I've had a whole summer to think about this. I read about it, too. This is not something that's our fault."

"I'm not talking about *our* fault," Dad jumped in immediately.

"What *are* you talking about, Arthur?"

"The only way Pete runs true to type is that he's always been a mama's boy! Half the time while Pete was growing up, you two were off in a corner talking French together, giggling, carrying on!"

Mom said, "Take me right home."

I said, "Let me off in the village. I don't want to go home. I had my arm around Jack because he's breaking up with Nicki!"

"Don't bother to explain anything to him," Mom said.

"That's right!" said Dad. "Keep me in the dark,

where I've been all the while *you* raised the family!"

"I'm getting out right now!" I said.

"Not in the pouring rain, Erick!" Mom said.

But I was out the door before she finished the sentence.

I could hear Dad shout, "Let him go!"

I went.

Thirteen

"YOU'RE SOAKING WET," Nicki said.

"I hitchhiked here."

"Through a driving rain just to be at my side?"

"Something like that."

There was a cigarette dangling from her lips, and behind her, down a long hall, I could see the bar, and a red neon sign that said "This Bud's For You!" . . . A couple of Siamese cats scurried past me.

"Come this way," she said. "That's Three, Six, and Nine who just went by. They were Mom's cats. My Siamese is named Scatter."

We made a right turn down the lobby, past Annabel's Resale Shop, Nicki walking ahead of me. She had on a pair of black stirrup pants and a huge gold sweater the color of her hair, black Capezios, and in her right ear two black plastic circle earrings.

"I'll dry your hair in my room," she said. "They're about to watch the game in the bar."

"My hair will dry."

"I want to dry it with my blower. You'll look less like a water rat. Do you ever blow dry your hair?"

"Of course not."

"Of course not," she said. "You don't know what to do with yourself. You'll like yourself, you'll see."

She led me up some spiral stairs past the front desk, saying, "Everything in this place is named after something of Edgar Allan Poe's. My mother? She believed she was a reincarnation of him, only she told most people she was just related to him way back."

"Once I memorized 'The Raven' for English," I said. " 'Quoth the Raven, "Nevermore." ' "

" 'Once upon a midnight dreary,' " she said.

" 'While I wandered, weak and weary,' " I said.

"It's *pondered*, not wandered. I *do* know my Poe!" she said. "I live right down here in the Dream Within A Dream suite. . . . Where were you, at church or something? You're so dressed up."

"St. Luke's, with my family."

"Welcome to my home," she said. "Forget the rest of this place—this is where I hang out."

To the left of the door there was a tarnished brass plaque that read: *All that we see or seem Is but a dream within a dream.*

"Bells, Bells, Bells is down the hall," she said, "and The Raven is next to that." She went ahead of me, turned around, and said, "Well, come on!" still smoking no hands.

The first thing I saw as I turned inside was an enormous poster of David Lee Roth. There were other, smaller posters covering all the walls: U2, David Byrne, Sting, Duran Duran, Wham!, Bruce Springsteen.

"Coat off!" she said, leaning over to grind out her cigarette in a seashell ashtray.

I took off my coat and she hung it over the back of a white wicker chair. A fat Siamese cat opened her crossed eyes to stare at me.

"Shirt off!" she said. "That's Scatter on the chair."

"My shirt's not that wet," I said.

"It's soaking wet. Off!" she said.

I hated taking off my shirt. I felt like the "Before" picture in a Nautilus ad. I never had the build Jack had, or the muscles. I had freckles on my shoulders. Jack was like Dill, always tan from summer, way into fall. God knows what I had on my back besides freckles, too.

She hung my shirt and tie on a wire hanger over the doorknob of her closet.

"Kick your shoes off, too," she said. "Shoes and socks."

"What are *you* going to take off?" I said.

"Anything you say," she said, and she took a small Gillette hand drier from the top of her bureau.

She pointed to an old brass bed with a white bed-spread. "Sit down. I'm going to plug this in over here."

Everything in the room was white—scatter rugs, table, desk, chairs, blinds, all white, and outside a thick white fog hovered against the windows, hiding the ocean, though you could hear its sounds. The room itself smelled the way things close to the sea do, sort of a salty, damp, and musty odor.

Right before she turned on the drier, I said, "Dill's in Norton, Massachusetts, this weekend looking over the Wheaton campus." I had no idea what made me say that.

She pointed the drier at me like someone holding a gun to my head.

"I don't care where Marian Dilberto is this week-end," she said flatly.

I laughed painfully. David Lee Roth gave me the eye from the wall.

I heard the sudden whir of the drier, felt her fingers in my scalp, and smelled that same perfume. First.

When she was finished, she handed me a small mir-ror from her dressing table and said, "Do you like yourself now?"

I nodded yes. I had to admit to myself I liked what I saw.

"Are you going to get stuck up now?" she said.

We were both grinning hard at each other. I was

doing it the way you do it when you can't stop yourself.

"You want me to take you on a tour of this place?" she said.

"Sure!"

"You want to follow me?" she said. "No, you don't need your shoes or your shirt."

"I'm half naked," I said. "Don't you have any guests?"

"Guests? Guests? What are guests?"

"Customers?"

"What are customers?" she said.

She reached for my hand and pulled me to my feet.

"You know how this place got its name? 'I was a child and she was a child, In this kingdom by the sea,' " she said; " 'But we loved with a love that was more than love—' "

" 'I and my Annabel Lee,' " I finished it for her. "I remember that from English too."

"What would you do without English?" she said.

We were smiling at each other that same way again.

Smiling . . . but I was thinking what the hell am I even doing here?

If that question was on her mind, she never asked it.

Tacky, shabby, shitty, going to rack and ruin—those were the only words to describe Kingdom By The Sea, yet I could imagine that once it had been a crazy, fantastic place: mysterious and silly and rare. All the suites, like hers and Bells, Bells, Bells; The Raven; Helen; and The Black Cat, faced the ocean, while ordinary rooms with baths faced the Montauk Highway, with a courtyard separating them. In the center of the courtyard there was an old fountain Nicki said hadn't worked in years, "But when it did, it was lucky, and people tossed pennies into it and made wishes. I loved that thing! I threw my whole allowance into it! When Daddy cleaned it out, I never took my pennies back because I thought my wishes wouldn't come true if I did." We were looking down on the fountain from a window in the hall on the third floor.

"What were your wishes?" I asked her.

"Oh, you know how kids are, what kids wish for."

"I don't know what kids like you wished for."

"Kids like me? I wasn't any different then."

"So what'd you wish for?"

"Things. A doll. A bicycle. What I wished for and never got was a white horse. I got that from 'Ride a cockhorse to Banbury Cross, To see a fine lady upon a white horse.' See, I was her. Rings on her fingers, bells on her toes, et cetera."

" 'She shall have music wherever she goes.' "

"English again?" She laughed.

Then she said, "If it wasn't pouring out, I'd take you down there so we could read the inscription on the fountain. My mother was into inscriptions, among other flawed things. The inscription reads *Thou wast that all to me, love, For which my soul did pine—A green isle in the sea, love, A fountain and a shrine.* . . . My mother and Daddy had this thing between them where the earth moves? She was a lot younger than he was, a good fifteen years younger. . . . Want to go swimming?"

"*Swimming?*"

"Inside," she said. "We've got a heated saltwater pool down the hall."

It was called City By The Sea. There was a mural of New York's skyline going all the way around the room, with this huge pear-shaped pool in the center. There were a lot of white wooden chairs with the paint peeling, minus their cushions, set around the pool, on a tile floor. Nicki went into the control room to get the filter and heat going, and I wondered if they'd added any chlorine to it lately; it looked a little too green.

"Is it going?" she shouted out to me. "I don't want to turn it up too high, because it makes the TV in the bar jump when the power's up."

"It's going!"

She came out and said, "See, they're all watching the Colts in the bar."

"I don't follow football. Just local football." I thought

of Jack. I thought, Jesus, what the shit am I doing here with Jack's girl?

"Daddy doesn't have any bonds to cash in even if I did want to go to college, which I don't. I just made that up. We're practically bankrupt here."

"A lot of people don't go to college."

"I made all that up about Daddy wanting to meet all of you before we all went into New York City, too."

"Okay."

We were both standing there staring down at the pool. The water was beginning to move.

"I knew that was what you all expected, that Daddy'd want to look you over."

"Well, we're not put into this world to live up to other people's expectations," I said. I'd seen that on some poster somewhere.

She put out the cigarette she was smoking in another seashell. "College would be more of the same. More pom-pom girls, more dumb crowds going everywhere together. Why does everyone travel around in packs?"

I was thinking, What the hell am I going to wear if we go swimming? I had jockeys on, and I knew what jockeys would look like wet.

"I don't know why everyone travels around in packs," I said.

"Like animals or something," she said.

"Like packs of dogs. Dog packs." I could just jump in in my pants.

"Like herds. Sheep."

"It's security or something," I said.

"Security. Is that what it is?" She reached down and pulled her sweater over her head.

I just stood there.

She didn't have a bra on.

"Come on," she said. "I'm not doing a striptease for your benefit. We're going swimming, aren't we?"

So we went swimming, naked, and after we swam around for a while, staying as far away from each other as possible, she swam underwater surfacing a heartbeat away from me, then putting her arms up around my neck, and I could feel her breasts against my chest.

"You're going to drown me," I said.

"Am I ever going to drown you!" she said. "Don't you want me to?"

Somehow we got down to the shallow end, where we could touch, and that was what we did. We touched.

I could feel the softness of her lips and her body, and hear the sound of the rain on the sunroof over us.

"I forgot to turn on the music," she said at one point. "I can flood this place with music."

"Well, I'm hearing something that sounds like music," I said.

"I'll put the real music on later," she said. "Much later . . . after I'm tired of you."

I don't remember it getting dark. It was just dark finally.

We sneaked through the halls carrying our clothes, shivering, running for her bed when we got down to her room, jumping under the covers wet, giggling, talking very softly to each other, though there was no reason to, almost whispering: It's so late, it's gotten so dark, nothing sentences said almost solemnly in low, gentle voices.

"What about your dad?" I said finally. I was thinking about my own, about Mom, too.

"Let me put a light on," she said. "Let me buzz down and tell him I'll be down soon."

"What if he finds me here?"

"He won't come up. He's on the bar." She snapped on a lamp. Scatter was sitting on the bureau, watching us with light-blue crossed eyes.

"Have you got a phone I can use?"

She pointed to it on the table beside the bed. "Come here first."

Then she said, "I'm going to have to change those wet sheets. Oh, don't go away, Erick. Not yet . . . not yet."

I finally said I'd better make a phone call. Yes, she said.

I knew Mom would be worried.

Nicki got up and threw on a robe, and shouted something through a speaker on the wall about being hungry enough to eat a horse. "Oh, that's what's on the menu tonight? Horsemeat? Well, good!" She laughed. . . . She said, "Who's been calling? *Who?*" and laughed again. Jack, I thought.

She said, "Make your call. Then I'll walk you down."

I pulled on my jockeys and my pants, and got into my shirt.

She brought my shoes and socks over to me, leaned down, and kissed me on the mouth.

I was trembling as I dialed.

Dad answered the phone.

"Erick? I'm sorry about my behavior." I was light years away from his behavior. "There's no excuse for it," he said. Then he came up with one. "This whole business is more upsetting to me than I care to admit to myself. . . . The Neanderthal Man called several times." He tried laughing it off.

"He probably just misses me," I said. "You know how it is, Dad."

"All right. I deserve that."

"Tell Mom I'll be there shortly."

Nicki put my tie around my neck, slapped my hands away from it, and said, "Let me tie it."

After she had it tied, she said, "Do you have to go?"

"I have to go."

We walked out into the hall and down the spiral staircase about as slowly as two people could walk. She asked me how I'd get home and I said I'd get home, not to worry.

In front of the door, I turned around and faced her. She had slippers on and the white robe, and I reached inside the robe and touched her.

"You want to get home, don't you? You won't get home that way."

I started to say something about Jack, something about how I didn't know how I could have let myself do what I did to Jack, but she shook her head no and put one finger to my lips, to hush me.

I caught her hand and then I let it go.

I turned back around and opened the door. I heard her say the rain had stopped, good, I wouldn't get wet. She snapped on floodlights.

When I was halfway down the walk, she came running toward me from behind, and I stopped when she called, "Erick? Wait!"

"What?"

I turned around and she caught hold of me, and we sort of spun around and around, hanging on to each other, laughing, then not laughing. "I hate for you to go!" she said. We stood there in the bright lights like people onstage in a play.

"I'll be back," I said.

I closed my eyes, holding her as hard as I could, and when I opened them, I saw the Mustang, stopped just at the drawbridge. He must have been on his way up the road when he spotted us.

"Jack," I said. "It's Jack," and I watched him back up, then turn around and take off.

Fourteen

THE SCHOOL WEEK began with a letter from Dill, taped to my locker.

Dear Erick,

Jack came by last night, and I guess I don't have to tell you what we talked about. Since you didn't even call to see if I was back from Massachusetts, I guess what Jack saw at Kingdom By The Sea says it all. I've known since we came back from New York that something was wrong, that something happened there to change you. I guess it's boring to be stuck with someone who doesn't put out, right? Well, you knew what to do about that, didn't you? The thing I can't get over isn't even what you did to us by running off to her, it's what you did to Jack! I might have forgiven you for going behind my back to make out with someone like her, if that's what you did, but I could never, ever forgive you for going behind Jack's back, going after the only girl he ever cared anything about. If

that's the kind of friend you are, then how could any-
one trust you?

I don't want anything more to do with you. In a
way I'm glad this happened senior year, since I can
now go on to Wheaton (if I get in, and it looks good!)
and not have anyone from the past to keep me from
enjoying the future. I hope you enjoy yours, Rudd,
but if I were you I wouldn't sleep well nights . . . but
maybe sex with The Slut will help you sleep.

Dill

That was the strangest week I ever spent at Seaville
High.

Overnight, Nicki and I became an instant couple,
but we were like the two new kids in some school
where we didn't even know anyone's name, left to
ourselves as word spread like a fire through dry grass
that I'd taken Jack's girl away from him.

On the one hand, I'd see Dill pass me in the halls
as though I wasn't there, and Jack looking everywhere
but at me, and I'd feel this incredible loneliness, like
I was the invisible man.

On the other hand, I'd see Nicki coming toward me,
wearing one of her goofy, great, beautiful outfits, a
yellow lace dress, say, with that nutty black-leather-
fringe jacket, the traffic accident on its back, and she'd
be smiling at me, and she was mine, so none of the
rest of it mattered. But it was definitely a high/low

game, and I tried to think of it as a game, though it was so intense sometimes I'd catch my breath, and long for the old familiar routines of senior year, being tight with one girl and one crowd, and having a long history with both, instead of all of it being new.

And always, there was Pete on my mind. Always the thought that if I ever needed Dill and Jack, the main ones in my life who knew what Pete was to me, it was then.

So it was back and forth, and I was down so low sometimes I felt like a complete stranger to myself, then *up*, soaring, lost somewhere with her, too high to care about the rest of it.

Nights when I wasn't working, I was out at Kingdom By The Sea, for as long as I could stay, in Dream Within A Dream, or swimming down in City By The Sea—a wave to Cap Marr, a word or two exchanged between us . . . and I remembered the first time she'd introduced me to him, he'd grinned and said, "A new one, Fickle Pickle? Well, what's your name? . . . Rudd? Don't let her make your name Mud, Rudd," laughing.

"This is different, Daddy!" Nicki told him. "So don't scare him off, hmmm? I'm not a fickle pickle anymore."

If anyone wasn't going to scare me off, it was her father. He was like this large, overgrown kid, cuddling the Siamese cats in his arms, giving them the run of the bar, strolling around in his Help Feed The People

T-shirt, with the visor cap tipped forward hiding his eyes. There were always girls years younger than he was nursing tequila sunrises on tall stools, while he watched sports on the TV up on the shelf over the bar, or talked with Toledo, who'd scare anyone off, he was so bad-tempered and big.

If a kid could dream up the perfect father for the girl he was dating, Cap would win hands down. He was mellowed out like someone with a horrendous pot habit; nothing seemed to ruffle his feathers, not our skinny-dipping in the pool, not my presence in her bedroom.

"He's in the midst of a major nervous breakdown because we're losing so much business?" Nicki said. "See, major disappointments make him real sweet."

"Maybe you'd have more business if you got rid of Toledo."

"Toledo looks worse than he is. It's just that fags get to him. He said seeing a fag walk in the bar was like seeing the first maggot crawl onto a dead body, like it was the end here. Toledo's been with this place since we started, so it's like his place, too. We've always had motorcycle guys, like Ski, or fishermen. It's always been a macho bar."

"Do fags bother you?" I asked her.

"*Me?* I'd love to make love to one. Change him? I bet I could!"

"What if he didn't want to change?"

Nicki laughed. "I'd let him dress up in my clothes. I'd help him be a real queen like Boy George. I'd play him *The Age of Consent*."

"I don't know *The Age of Consent*."

"It's Bronski Beat's album. They're this Scottish trio who're gay. They all wear pink triangles like the ones homosexuals were forced to wear by the Nazis. They have this song 'Smalltown Boy,' about a gay kid who has to get away from his family and his town."

"But what if a fag isn't swishy; what if he looks like any other guy?"

"Then that's such a waste," Nicki said. "That's just a waste of manpower, isn't it?"

I let the subject drop there.

That Friday afternoon when I got home from school, there was a SAAB 900 Turbo in the driveway, with JJ-SCIFI on the license plate.

Mom met me at the door to tell me Jim Stanley and Pete were in the living room having coffee. She said Oscar'd been put to sleep.

I ducked into the kitchen to get control of myself. I blew my nose and got a Coke from the refrigerator. I was standing at the sink, trying to keep back the tears, when Pete came in.

"Why didn't you at least let me say good-bye to him?" I said.

"We got here at two," Pete said. "The vet closes at

four. . . . You knew I was going to do it this week."

"I didn't know when. I guess I'm not grown-up enough to be told that, either."

Pete ignored that. He said, "I thought it was *my* responsibility, Ricky."

"Yours and Jim's?"

"Ricky, Jim was just kind enough to drive me out."

"God, Pete, he was my dog, too!"

Pete looked thinner every time I saw him. I felt rotten for shouting at him.

He put his arm around my shoulder. "I held Oscar while he got the shot. He went very peacefully."

"Poor Oscar Wilde." I smiled up at Pete. "I'm sorry I blew up at you."

"Forget it. Come on in and see Jim. We can't stay for dinner."

Pete had on a herringbone tweed jacket, gray flannels, a white shirt, and a striped tie.

"Why are you so dressed up?"

"I stopped in to see Reverend Shorr. Mom's going to need some support, eventually."

"You told him?"

"That's why I went to see him."

"Does Dad know you told him?"

"Just you and Jim know. Mom doesn't even know. I want somebody outside of family to be ready to help Mom."

"What did old Snore say?"

"He said how fond he was of Mom. Then he started talking about the way homosexuality was treated in the Bible. He said something about anyone who reaches back four thousand years and pulls forward a law code written for nomads in the desert, and claims it applies here and now, isn't being honest with the scriptures."

"Then he's not against it?"

"He's certainly not for it," Pete said. "He was treating the subject intellectually. You know Snore. He was quoting Leviticus and what Paul said in Romans, questioning the interpretation." Pete sank his hands into his trousers and said, "Ricky? Mom always acts like she's solid as a rock, like nothing surprises her, but there's a lot of stuff coming down she doesn't even imagine."

"Like what, Pete?"

"Okay. I had to make a deal with Southworth. Legally, they can't fire me because I have AIDS. But I knew they wouldn't want me around. I need my medical benefits, and I've earned them. So I offered to take a leave of absence with a month's notice. . . . They accepted the offer, providing that I left that day."

I started to say something, but Pete held up his hand. "Wait, there's more. . . . I told a friend of mine in the apartment building. At least I *thought* she was

my friend. I'm going to lose the sublet. She's circulating a petition to get me out. It's not my apartment,
so I can't fight it. . . . I'm a little like a leper, pal. I'm
a lot like one."

"God, Pete, I'm sorry."

"It's just the tip of the iceberg, I'm afraid. You'll
see soon enough, and I'm sorry as hell I'm bringing
this down on the family. . . . There's something else.
I'm not going to San Francisco with Jim."

"Did Dad talk you out of it?"

"No. Jim's deal came through for the TV series. It's
not a good time for him to chase off to San Francisco,
or for me to go to the coast. I'm going to put myself
in Phil Kerin's hands."

"Good, Pete! Dad says he's the best!"

"So I'll be around. Here."

"In Seaville?"

"In Seaville," Pete said. " 'Home is the place where,
when you have to go there, They have to take you in.'
Five dollars says you don't know who wrote that."

"Dad?"

Pete laughed and mussed up my hair. "Come on in
and see Jim."

Fifteen

JIM STANLEY stood up and shook my hand.

One of the things I'd learned about Nicki was that she was never happy until she figured out what celebrity you looked like. She said I was a curly-haired version of singer Roddy Frame from Aztec Camera, but I'd never seen or even heard of Roddy Frame. . . . Jim Stanley, Nicki'd say, was a younger Richard Chamberlain. He was one of those really poised guys, with all the right, polite gestures, the type any mother'd love her daughter to bring home and meet the family.

But Pete had brought him home.

I don't know what the guy could have done right under those circumstances. I know I didn't like him calling me Ricky (only Pete called me that), and Mom looked away every time he gave Pete an affectionate nudge or tap on the knee, and every time he said "we" this and "we" that, which was a lot of times.

The touching got to me, too. Jim Stanley was a toucher. It looked like the same innocent contact Jack and I had had together back when we were still speaking, but somehow it bothered me. I kept wishing they'd sit farther away from each other on the couch, too.

For a while we sat around talking about the new series Jim was writing for NBC.

Mom said, "Erick wants to get into film work, too."

"Maybe," I said.

"N.Y.U. has a great film school," Jim said. "Joel Coen went there. He and his brother did *Blood Simple* and *The XYZ Murders*. Great stuff!"

"I doubt that Dad's going to approve of film school," said Pete.

"Ah, yes," Jim said, "there's Himself to contend with."

Mom gave him a look. She said, "Mr. Rudd's always been open to suggestion."

"Just like the Pope is." Pete grinned.

Both Pete and Jim thought that was pretty funny, but Mom didn't like it. It was okay for Pete and me to kid about Dad, but Mom didn't want an outsider joining in on the joke.

I was remembering when we were kids, and Dad was laying down the law, Pete called him "O Infallible!" I was so much younger than Pete, I didn't even know how to pronounce "infallible," much less what it meant. It came out of my mouth "O Full of Bull."

Pete must have read my mind. He looked over at me and said, "O Full of Bull's pushing hard for Erick to get an M.B.A."

"Pete?" Mom said. "Why don't you get Jim another cup of coffee?"

She wanted to change the subject, get it off Dad.

Jim said no thanks, but he thought Pete could use a sandwich.

Mom was about to get up when Pete said he couldn't eat anything.

"An eggnog then," Jim said. "How about an eggnog?"

"Nothing. Thanks, anyway."

"Pete?" Jim said in a scolding tone.

Mom looked out the window.

"I don't think I can get anything down," Pete said.

"I'll make it the way you like it," Jim said, "not too sweet, with a jigger of rum. Mrs. Rudd? You have eggs, vanilla, milk, and a little light rum?"

"Yes, I'll make it." Mom started to get up, but Jim was on his feet.

"I know how he likes it," Jim said. *"Moi, j'ai pris charge."*

"Fais ce que tu dois," Pete said, which only meant "do your duty," but Mom looked like she'd been insulted. That had always been her little game with Pete, the quips back and forth in French. Her crossed leg

was swinging the way an angry cat's tail flailed the air.

"I'll help you find the rum," Pete said, and he got up and followed Jim toward the kitchen.

After they'd gone, I said, "How come Pete's not going to the coast?"

"Jim shares an apartment with a friend. The friend doesn't want Pete there."

"Because of AIDS?"

"That's probably why, yes."

"Is Pete upset about it?"

"Stop asking me how Pete feels, Erick. I haven't a clue. Jim tells me more than Pete does—more than I want to know, too. About everything."

"Like what?"

"Pete's had things before. Hepatitis."

"A lot of people get hepatitis."

"Other things. Worse things. Things he's never told us about."

"What'd you expect, Mom? That he'd announce to you and Dad he'd picked up clap or something? I wouldn't either, unless I *had* to!"

"And Jim said Pete hadn't really had many relationships. Jim said not what you could call relationships—until Jim came along."

"Pete got around. He told me he did."

"Oh, Pete got around all right. I asked Jim *why* Pete was so prone to those things . . . infections . . . and

Jim said Pete didn't ever stay with one person very long. Jim said there are some gay men who can't, because they grew up hiding what they were, never learning to socialize with each other, except in bars . . . at *baths*. It's all so sordid!"

"Then don't ask Jim stuff."

"Maybe Pete wouldn't be in this mess if I'd asked Pete some questions a long time ago."

"Have another heaping teaspoon of guilt," I said.

"Jim just comes out with these statements: Some gay men have been with more than they could count . . . more than they could count."

"Well, if Pete'd been with more girls than he could count, if it was more girls than he could count—"

"It wasn't, though," Mom said bitterly.

"But what if it was? Then it'd be okay. Dad's always telling Pete and me to sow our wild oats, right? Marriage is forever, right? So do a lot of playing around."

"Your father was talking about men and women and marriage."

"But he's always telling us to play around a lot!"

"I don't want to continue with this conversation. . . . I miss Oscar so much, I could cry."

"I miss him too."

"Jim took me aside and told me Pete was really upset about Oscar, that Oscar was a symbol of a whole part of Pete's life that was ending. He said Pete was putting up a front for me, but Pete was devastated, so they weren't going to stay for dinner, because he wanted to get Pete home. I said Pete *is* home."

"Jim's in a no-win situation here," I said.

"*Moi, j'ai pris charge,*" Mom said icily. "His French accent leaves a lot to be desired, too. . . . Am I being bitchy?"

"Yeah, very bitchy. . . . I'm not going to be here for dinner, Mom."

"I have a rehearsal, anyway. Are you going over to Dill's?"

"Not tonight."

"Is everything all right between you and Jack? I haven't seen him around lately."

"Everything's fine," I said. I wasn't going to lay *my* problems on her, on top of everything else.

"Honey? I don't want to keep talking about this thing, but I've left a sheet of instructions up on your bureau. With Pete coming back to live with us, there are some precautions we all have to take."

"Okay," I said. "I'll read it. . . . When's Pete moving back in?"

"As soon as Jim goes back to the coast," Mom said. "I just can't think of them as a couple, can you?"

"No, not really."

"It's something wrong in us that we can't, isn't it?" Mom said.

I said, "Just stop thinking about what's wrong in

you, Mom. You're doing your best to handle it."

"You're handling it too well," Mom said. "It worries me."

When Pete and Jim came back from the kitchen, Pete said he felt a lot better. Jim said, *"See?"*

We stood around for a while saying good-bye.

Mom offered to drive in her station wagon when Pete was ready to move his stuff out to Seaville.

"I'm giving Pete my SAAB while I'm on the coast," Jim told her. "He doesn't have any furniture to move, thank God. He can probably get everything into the SAAB."

"I hope you know what you're doing, the way Pete drives."

"I know what I'm doing, Mrs. Rudd," Jim said.

"Good luck with your new series, Jim!" I said.

"I'm trying to talk Pete into shelving *The Skids* for a while, to help me with some scripts. I never thought I'd collaborate B.P."

"B.P.?" I had to ask.

"Before Pete," Jim said.

After they roared off, Mom began rearranging the living room furniture. She always did that when she was unhappy and anxious. I went upstairs and got into the shower. When I got out, I reached under the bathroom cabinet for Mom's hair drier. I don't know why I didn't want her to hear me using it, but I didn't, so I turned on the tub water.

I watched myself in the mirror while I blew my hair dry.

I remembered Nicki's voice purring, "Do you like yourself now? Are you going to get stuck up now?"

I tried not to think about the sheet of instructions Mom had left on my bureau, beginning *1. Kitchen and bathroom facilities may be shared with others, but not toothbrushes or bars of soap, or . . .*

I didn't let myself get into it, but turned my thoughts around to Nicki, and the way she made me feel, and the best things about her: her nerve. Her great war against *them*. The way she let me know she wanted me, too, so that I never felt like some horny high school kid out to get his rocks off. How easy it was for me to say I love you.

It was not saying it that was hard. I said it and said it.

Once she asked me, "When did you know you loved me?"

I couldn't think when it was. I said, "Last Sunday afternoon."

"Not until then?"

"When did you know?"

"At your brother's place, when we talked, while they were in the kitchen. I thought, Oh no! I'm with the wrong guy."

"Why did you love me?"

"See, I don't think you can ever know why. I don't

think it's because you're redheaded and cute and I can talk to you. I think it's karma. My mother said everything was fate. Karma. Or it's chemistry. I could smell a dozen different closets full of clothes and pick yours out. You *smell* good to me."

"I want to give you the world!" I said. Things like that came out of my mouth all week. I guess the clichés about love got to be clichés because there was no other way to act or feel. You just expanded, said things you never did before, made all kinds of new moves as easily as if all your life you'd been at it. It was like coming into money suddenly or being discovered by some talent scout and becoming an overnight star.

That afternoon on my way home from school, I'd seen a little white china horse in the window of Seaville Antiques. I'd remembered she'd wished for a white horse once and never gotten it. I'd bought it for her. Across a card I'd written: *Nicki, You shall have music wherever you go. Love, Eri.* That was the name she'd come to call me. I liked it that she called me something as new as she was to me. . . . I realized I'd never bought a gift for Dill unless there was an occasion for it. We'd never given each other special names.

On my way out of the house, I overheard Mom in the kitchen talking with Mrs. Tompkins. I heard her say Pete was sick with AIDS. Did Mrs. Tompkins know what AIDS was?

"Of course I know what that is. But not Peter. Peter's not . . . Peter's not . . ."

I let myself out the front door and headed off to Kingdom By The Sea.

Sixteen

By THE TIME Pete moved back to Seaville, Kingdom By The Sea was my second home. Nicki worked in Annabel's Resale Shop afternoons when I worked at the bookstore, but other afternoons we spent together in Dream Within A Dream, or walking down on the dunes, or swimming at City By The Sea. I'd go home for dinner, and then go back there until ten or eleven at night. Nicki never wanted to go anywhere. She said going places changed her the same way alcohol did certain people. She said once she got away from Kingdom By The Sea, she became different.

"Anyway, we don't need other people," she said. "Do we need them, do you think, or are we perfect as we are?"

"Perfect as we are," I'd answer, but sometimes I'd wish I could show her off, go places and be seen with her, talk about her to someone. . . . And sometimes I missed Jack so much, I felt like bawling.

I found a ten-foot green vinyl float shaped like a crocodile, with black spots and big white teeth, at The Seaville Beach Shop. Nicki loved that thing. We'd ride it together in the pool, with songs like R.E.O. Speedwagon's "Can't Fight This Feeling" blasting over the speakers. She named the crocodile after Kevin Cronin, who'd written that song. "It's our song, Eri," she said, and she'd found a little gold crocodile that'd come into the resale shop with some estate jewelry, and fixed it on a gold chain for me to wear around my neck.

One early November night we were hanging on to Kevin Cronin down near the shallow end of the pool, while a wine salesman who was staying at KBTS did swan dives at the deep end. Nicki was fooling around, taking the crocodile around my neck into her mouth, and I finally began the conversation I'd been working up to all day.

"You know what I'd like to give you?"

"I know what you'd like to give me." She laughed.

"Be serious. . . . Senior rings come in next week."

At Seaville High we got our rings in November, so we'd have a longer time to wear them before school was out. We celebrated getting them at a dance on Thanksgiving Eve. Some seniors exchanged rings at that dance. That dance was a bigger event than the Senior Prom at Seaville High. It was THE affair of the year.

"You know what I'd never wear? A senior ring," Nicki said. "I didn't even order one. I think it looks moronic to wear your high school ring once you're out of high school."

"What about wearing mine while you're in high school?"

"Oh, no, here it comes!" she said.

"Here what comes?" I said, but I knew there was no fooling her.

"Eri, what do you want? To go to that Ring Dance?"

"Maybe I just want you to wear my ring."

"You want me to go to that thing with you, don't you?"

"Okay," I said. "But not really *go* to it, just drop in at it."

"Just get all dressed up and get in that line of Noah's Ark nerds who go two by two into that big plastic ring! What would I give you?"

"You don't have to give me anything. I'd give you my ring."

"Jack will be at that thing. Jack and Dill and all of them!"

"Not Jack," I said. "Not Jack at a dance if he can help it!"

"Everybody else, though. Baaaa! Baaaaaa! Baaaaaaaa!"

I grabbed her and ducked her, and when I let her up, I said, "You going with me?"

"*Pas du tout.*" She shook her head no. "That's French," she said, putting her arms around my neck, her mouth coming toward mine. "So's this."

One night, out at Kingdom By The Sea, we were watching home movies, which was a passion of Cap's, I found out. He loved staring up at the old days in the dark bar, wiping his eyes unashamedly, saying things to Nicki like, "Remember that summer, honey? We got Scatter that summer, and your mommy had that seance and got in touch with Uncle Dave through Scatter?"

"I never really believed she got in touch with Uncle Dave," said Nicki, and she said in an aside to me, "Uncle Dave was killed in Vietnam."

"Oh, it was Dave talking through her all right," Cap said. "She couldn't have made up all that stuff herself. All the details of the fighting over in Nam? Your mommy didn't know diddly-damn about war!"

They'd go on about things like that, and I'd sit with Scatter on my lap. She'd taken a liking to me, although every chance she got, she took her paw and swatted the little white horse I'd given to Nicki off the bureau in Nicki's room. Nicki'd named it High Horse. It was on its side on the rug more than it was on the bureau, and Nicki'd say, "Scatter's jealous of High Horse, I think."

This night we were all watching the home movies.

I saw Cap when he was much younger, and I saw Nicki's mother, Annabel, who looked much younger than Cap. There were all sorts of shots of them there at Kingdom By The Sea, when it was first built and not yet gone to pot.

They were such a good-looking couple. I watched them feeding each other watermelon slices at a picnic on the dunes, then chasing each other through waves at the edge of the ocean, and playing badminton in shorts in the courtyard, two tanned, happy-looking young people, Annabel not much older than Nicki and me.

Finally little Nicole came into the pictures. There were Cap and Annabel holding her up so she could put a penny into the fountain. Then there they were with her walking between them, suddenly holding her while she swung from their hands, her tiny legs off the ground, laughing, with her hair golden in the sunlight, blue skies above, everything going for the three of them . . . and they looked it.

I held Nicki's hand while we watched her life spin by in the dark bar, another night of almost no customers. Toledo working crossword puzzles at the desk outside, Cap sipping draft Bud and bumming Merits from Nicki. Their cigarette smoke curled up above us in a blue haze, as Nicki grew up before my eyes, while beside me she'd say things like, "I loved that little bike! I thought I was SOMETHING on that thing! I'd run right over rocks and let the tires lift off the ground like it was a dirt bike? And remember the time the tire just blew up, Daddy?"

"You were bawling like you'd seen the bogeyman!" Cap said.

"Well, I didn't know what'd happened! See, it just blew up after I ran the thing over a curb!"

It was one of the few nights at Kingdom By The Sea when the young girls who were like Cap's groupies weren't hanging around, when rock wasn't roaring out of the speakers, and Nicki wasn't telling me the life stories of Van Halen, Billy Idol, Journey, Kiss, et cetera.

Then suddenly there was a new face up there, and as I saw Nicki's eyes watching it in all the scenes, my heart turned over and sank.

It was Ski. Ski sitting on his Kawasaki, with her behind him, messing up his black hair with her long fingers. Ski sitting in the dunes bare chested with a piece of elephant grass between his teeth while she grabbed it away and put her mouth against his. Then Ski carrying her into the ocean with her feet kicking, laughing up at him.

"There's our boy!" Cap laughed.

"He's not my boy anymore," and Nicki squeezed my hand.

But I was crushed, watching them together, her eyes looking into Ski's so lovingly, the way they sometimes looked at me, almost bringing tears to mine, they said so much . . . now up there on the screen saying the same things, the same way, to Ski.

I got into a panic.

I cut out early. I figured Nicki didn't even know the state I was in, probably believed me when I said I had to study for the English quiz the next day.

I walked along the highway for a long time in the cold autumn night before I started seriously hitchhiking.

Lots of nights when I got back from KBTS, I went up to see Pete. He'd eventually moved into Mrs. Tompkins' old apartment over the garage.

Mrs. Tompkins had tried. But the first night Pete had dinner at home, Mrs. Tompkins had served his on a yellow plastic plate from a set we kept in our family picnic basket. She'd said, "Wouldn't it be better if we kept Peter's dishes separate?" . . . And after that Mom found her doing Pete's sheets and pillowcases by hand in a tub filled with Tide and Clorox, in the basement, wearing rubber gloves. She'd said no matter what the sheet of instructions had said, she didn't think Pete's things should be laundered with everyone else's. It went on and on, and when Mom said we weren't going to live that way, that we'd take all the necessary precautions but not go overboard, Mrs. Tompkins broke down and admitted that her daughter wanted her to quit, twenty years with us or not! Mrs. Tompkins was terrified, too.

"She told her daughter," Dad said wearily, "so now it starts."

"Her daughter lives in Ohio," Mom said, "and Mrs. Tompkins is going there to live. So nothing starts. . . . Something ends. Mrs. Tompkins was like one of the family."

But it launched Dad on another lecture to all of us, about making sure we didn't confide in *anyone*.

"Eventually, we've got to figure out how to explain Pete's being here," Mom said. "Erick hasn't even had Jack to the house since Pete's been here. Or Dill!"

"That hasn't got anything to do with Pete," I said. "Jack and I had a fight about something else."

"About what?" Mom wanted to know.

"Just school stuff, Mom."

"What are you telling Dill?" Dad asked me.

"Nothing," I said. "Dill's so busy with graduation plans and yearbook stuff and all the rest, she doesn't even know Pete's here."

I let it go at that. There were a lot of reasons I didn't want to fill them in on my life at that point. I didn't want to admit I'd taken Jack's girl. I didn't want Mom nagging me about when she'd meet Nicki, knowing how Nicki felt about family-around-the-table crap. But mostly, I couldn't bear to tell Pete that a whole new part of my life had started, just as Pete's was beginning to end.

Although Pete often said casually, in conversation, that he was dying, Dad and Mom and I acted like we hadn't heard him. Mom would always change the subject, fast.

But none of us could deny what we saw with our own eyes. Pete's hair was thinning, due to chemotherapy. There were dark circles under his eyes. Sometimes he slept whole afternoons away, he was so weak. There were ugly, purple Kaposi's sarcoma lesions on parts of his body.

When I got up to his apartment, Pete was in the shower. He hollered out at me that he wouldn't be long. Pete had become a night owl more and more, getting up after we had dinner, going to bed when we got up.

There was an unfinished short story on his desk, and I shouted in to ask him if it was okay for me to look at it.

"If you want to! It's not worked out, though!"

It was called "The Sweet Perfume of Good-bye."

It was about a world where there was no fragrance except an exquisite perfume a dying person exuded a year before it was his time to die. That was the only scent in that world, this incredible and seductive odor. . . . It was as far as Pete had gotten, but it got me right behind the eyes.

Pete came out of the bathroom with a towel wrapped around him, bone skinny, the purple KS lesions showing on his arms and legs.

"I like the story so far," I managed, and I told myself I wasn't going to break down, wasn't going to lay that kind of trip on Pete.

"Making the better of the bitter," Pete said. "I can't seem to stick with my Skids, or write anything but short stories."

"But wouldn't everybody be busy murdering everybody else, so they could smell that perfume?"

"There's no murder in that world," Pete said. "No illness. Death is thought of as the great change, and it comes randomly to people at different times. But a year before the death there's this perfume, the only one in that world. I'm still working on it." Pete slipped into some shorts and began pulling on old cords. "You're home early. How's Dill?"

"She's the same," I said.

While Pete started talking about some Thanksgiving plans Mom was making, I thought of what it must have been like for Pete when he was my age and couldn't talk about his personal life. I was getting a small taste of that, living in my own private little world, squelching every instinct I had to talk about Nicki, or the breakup between Dill and me, or Jack. . . . I felt really distanced from everyone, so much so that it took me a while to hear what Pete was telling me. Mom was planning a *surprise* party for Pete on Thanksgiving Day?

"Then how do you know about it?" I said.

"Jim knows I don't like surprises. He told me so I could stop her if I want to. I want to, but I can't." He pulled on a shirt. "She's invited Jim, Marty and Shawn, his lover, and Stan and Tina Horton."

"Do you want me to talk to her about it?"

"No. What can you say? She's trying, Jim's trying. Everyone's trying. How the hell can I object to that? . . . Last night she said she realized how hard it is for me to be separated from Jim. It isn't that hard. It's almost a relief, but she wouldn't understand that."

"See"—I began sounding like Nicki—"none of us even knows what you feel for him, if you miss him, that kind of junk."

"He's a friend," Pete said. "I don't feel that way about him, Ricky. I think Jim's talking himself into feeling that way about me. He doesn't want to walk out on me now. If I hadn't come down with AIDS, we'd have just been good buddies after we came back from Europe."

"Maybe he really does feel something, though," I

said. "What if you're wrong that he's just forcing himself to stick by you because you've got AIDS?" I kept
remembering Jim Stanley's saying "we" in conversation, how he'd insisted on making the eggnog, the way
he'd touched Pete from time to time in the living room,
and how he'd said B.P. . . . Before Pete. . . . I think
I felt a little teed off at Pete, and I know I thought of
Dad's saying Pete never finished things he started.

Pete walked over to the couch where I was sitting.
He sat down beside me. "You know how you're always
worrying because you can't say 'I love you,' Ricky?"

"Yeah." I wished to hell I could tell him all that was
over, and all the rest. But I still couldn't see myself
taking up Pete's time with the little-brother-in-the-
throes-of-first-passion bit, while he was trying not to
puke after his weekly chemotherapy, writing his will,
staffing an AIDS hotline in New York weekends, listening to one horror story after the other.

"I worried about saying those words in a different
way," Pete said. "I'd no sooner say the words than the
feeling would fly out the window. I think relationships
scared the hell out of me. I guess it was because if one
lasted, I'd have to face a lot of shit I didn't want to.
I'd be seen with one guy all the time. How could I
explain that to the family, and straight friends, and
people from Southworth?"

A new tape by Art Ensemble that Jim'd sent Pete
was playing softly in the background.

Pete said, "Even just a few minutes ago, I couldn't say that I don't love Jim. I had to say that I don't feel *that way* about him. I've always had a problem being openly gay, or talking with straights about my gay feelings."

Pete sank back against the cushions. "That's probably why I couldn't get used to being with just one person," he said. "I couldn't go through all that. I'm not saying that I deliberately set out to sabotage every relationship I ever had, but I think a lot of those feelings were in operation. . . . So I never stayed with anyone very long."

"That's really lousy, isn't it?" I said.

Pete shrugged. "I never used to think so. I never thought that much about it. I just told myself I was young, I was this sexy guy. The more the merrier."

"Then it wasn't lousy," I said, "if you were happy."

"Now I think about a lot of things I never thought about before. But I don't look back on my life and say I should have done this, or I shouldn't have done that, any more than anyone else dying probably does. You don't die at my age without regrets, or without thinking how you might have done things differently."

I let out this long sigh, and Pete reached over and squeezed my knee.

"It's okay," he said. "We can talk about my dying."

"Maybe you can," I said, and my voice broke.

"I hope the two of us can talk about anything, Ricky."

"Okay," I said, "but now I'm going to let you finish that story," and I got up to go. I was too close to blurting out I'm getting laid, I've lost Jack, don't die, I need you, too close to just covering my eyes with my hands and bawling.

Pete said, "You know, Mom worries that you're handling all this too well."

"Mom thinks you're going to enjoy her Thanksgiving surprise, too," I said.

Pete chuckled. "Well, I'm going to try not to disappoint her."

When I got back to my room, Nicki called.

"Yes," she said.

"What does 'yes' mean?"

"Yes, I'll go to the dumb Ring Dance. I even know what I'm going to wear."

"How come you changed your mind?"

"How come you gave me a real nothing kiss when you left here tonight? You were bummed because of all the pictures of Ski and me together. . . . You want to hear what I'm going to wear, Eri? You know those white dogs with the black spots?"

"Dalmatians?"

"I've got these dalmatian-dotted stockings brand-new someone dropped off at the shop today. I'm going to wear *them*."

"I've got a ring you're going to wear."

"I just wish I didn't have to go to that cattle call to get it. See, I'm not into being a cow, Eri, or a sheep."

I did my Martin Short imitation. "It will surely be a delight. Because, like, it's a very decent thing to have this tradition, I must say. I'm going mental just thinking about it, and I'm doomed as doomed can be if you say no, no question about that. Showing you off at such a decent occasion, give me a break, I'm ecstatic!"

"ZZZZZZZZZZZ," she said.

Seventeen

THANKSGIVING EVE, Pete said, "Never mind trying to get Dad's car now. You'll be late. Take Jim's SAAB to the dance."

We could hear Mom and Dad shouting at each other, all the way down in the kitchen.

"I don't give a damn if they *don't!*" Mom said.

"They're my *family!*" Dad said.

"What's Pete?" Mom yelled back.

"What are they fighting about?" I asked Pete.

"You mean this time?" Pete sighed. "Dad finally told Grandpa Rudd I have AIDS, and Grandpa Rudd says he and Grandma won't come for Christmas."

"Good!" I said. "We'll actually have a Christmas where Grandpa Rudd isn't on Dad's back about everything!"

Pete didn't answer me. He was busy cleaning up his room for Jim's arrival later that night. Marty and Shawn were staying at some motel. Stan and Tina

Horton were driving out from New York for Thanksgiving dinner, then going back the same day.

I knew how depressed Pete seemed lately. I tried to leave on a light note, tried to make a joke about the battle going on under us. "I don't feel right about borrowing Jim's SAAB," I said, "but I'll make the big sacrifice, since I don't want to interrupt our parents' marvelous dialogue."

Pete only said, "I don't feel right about using Jim's car, either," gnawing on his own guilty bone, tossing me the keys, "but he'd want you to take it, Ricky."

I caught the keys and gave Pete a wave, running down the stairs, to the garage, out the side door to the driveway where the SAAB was parked.

I thought about other nights I'd gone to something at school, how I'd always waited for Jack to honk, how we'd always doubled for those things, and talked on our way to get our dates and after we'd dropped them off.

Sometimes when I was with Nicki in bed, I'd feel this strange sadness when I remembered the old days when Jack would say things like "When that happens, it means a girl's excited, right? So how does *she* get over it, if we stop in the middle of everything?"

Now, when I had all the answers, Jack wasn't there with the questions. There wasn't anyone anywhere with questions: just Nicki and me in our own cocoon.

I passed Reverend Snore chugging up our street in his old Chevy that all the parishioners, including Dad, complained gave St. Luke's a tacky image, on his way for a backgammon game with Pete.

Snore's visits were a sore point with Dad.

Once Dad said that was a great idea Mom had to tell Snore, just like her, just like her!

"*I* told Snore!" Pete said.

"Don't cover up for your mother!" Dad insisted.

"If Mom *had* told Snore, why would it be just like her?" I wanted to know.

"Just like her to involve the community in our private affairs!" Dad said. "Just like her now, to let you and Pete lie for her!"

We couldn't seem to convince Dad she hadn't lied, so I finally just tossed in, "Well, we're all a little mendacious lately, aren't we?" (I'd been reading *Cat on a Hot Tin Roof* for English. I'd gotten "mendacious" from Big Daddy's speeches in that play. I'd liked the sound of the word.)

I'd said that mendacity was our way of life, lately.

Dad had given me a crack across the head. First time ever.

I just sat there, trying to stop the tears from coming, while Mom rushed to put her arms around me.

"We have a full-blown crisis here!" Dad shouted. "I won't take his mouth!"

Mom said, "You never understood survival humor, never, Arthur!"

"Another of my failings!" Dad said. "I'll add it to the list, along with your judgment that my parents are middle-class ignoramuses, and the only reason I made The Hadefield Club is because *your* parents got me in!"

We were coming apart at the seams.

So I was glad when I saw Nicki standing by the front desk at Kingdom By The Sea, kibitzing with Toledo, rolling her cigarette around between her teeth.

She was wearing the dalmatian-dotted stockings with high black heels, some kind of black off-the-shoulder corset dress, with beads and crosses and chains, her crucifix earrings in her right ear, and black lace fingerless gloves. She had on the rhinestone ankle bracelet, and over her shoulder the jacket with the traffic accident on the back.

She had a bow in her hair with the same dalmatian pattern, and super-long false eyelash wings. And First. She smelled of that scent that had become so familiar to me, so her to me.

I waited until we got inside the SAAB to tell her something I dreaded telling her. Way back in September, when the seniors had ordered their rings, I'd ordered mine in Dill's size, as a surprise, with Dill's initials and mine inside.

Nicki was sitting close to me, with one hand under my thigh, the radio playing Julian Lennon's latest, while I broke the news.

She reacted the way she always did when I told her something important, completely opposite from how I thought she would. She clapped her hands together and said she just *loved* it, couldn't wait to wear it now!

"It's so dark and flawed, you couldn't give me anything more marvelous, Eri! I wish I could wear it inside out!"

After we parked the SAAB and walked toward the gym, Nicki tossed her Merit over her shoulder and hung tightly to my arm. "Here we go down the gangplank. Watch out for all the sharks, Eri!"

The first thing you were supposed to do, if you were giving someone a ring at the Ring Dance, was get your assigned place in the march.

Nicki sauntered into the girls' john to comb her hair while I walked up to the front table to pick up our number.

That was when I found myself face to face with Dill. She was sitting at the table with some other seniors.

She'd let her hair grow out. She was in white. She looked up at me.

"Hi, Dill."

She said, "Oh, you're going to be in the march?"

I nodded. "Are you?"

"Hardly."

There were blue and silver lights bobbing across our faces, while Wham! sang their old number "Careless Whisper" over the speakers.

Parental Guidance, the band that was playing for the dance, was just beginning to go up onstage.

"I like your hair," I told Dill.

"Then I'll always wear it this way," she said sarcastically.

"Dill," I said. I don't know what I would have said if she'd let me finish.

"You're number nine," she said, "after Todd Greenwald and Mildred Gregory." Ice could have formed around her words.

She started writing out the ticket.

A guitarist from the band began practicing a few cords as the speakers went off and other members of Parental Guidance slipped into place.

The guitarist was warming up with an old Beatles song.

I shouldn't have said, "Hey, maybe Gustavo Quintero's showed up after all these years."

"Don't," Dill said flatly.

I tried again to mumble something about being friends, about being sorry, but I was tripping over my own attempt at sincerity, mocking it inside, the way

I knew Dill would if I ever got out the words. At the same time I caught a fleeting glimpse of dalmatian spots running by, throwing me off altogether. I looked over my shoulder, but Nicki'd disappeared into the crowd.

When I glanced back at Dill, she had that crooked smile. "She's lighted on Roman now, up by the dance stand," Dill said.

I tried grinning, shrugging. "You make her sound like a mosquito."

"More like a flea," Dill said coldly. "Mosquitoes glide, almost gracefully. Fleas hop. From person to person."

"Well, Dill," I said, "you haven't lost your bite, either."

"I haven't *lost* anything, Rudd," said Dill. "You'll be the ninth couple." She handed me the ticket.

I took it and headed down the dance floor toward Nicki. Roman Knight, in a long black trenchcoat, carrying a black cane, and wearing one skull earring, was barking down at Nicki's legs.

I rescued her. We were the first couple out on the floor as Parental Guidance began playing.

"See, that sleazeball doesn't like me at all," Nicki said. "Barking at me! What's his problem?"

"You've got on dogs' legs," I said. "When you put them on, didn't you know someone would bark at them?"

"It's more than that," she insisted. "It's him. It isn't that."

"It's that!" I said firmly. "Just keep dancing."

We danced. She was a fantastic dancer. She'd do things to music I'd never seen anyone do.

When the floor got very crowded, after several numbers, she said she wanted to go out to the SAAB and have her "nicotine fix."

We stayed there awhile after she smoked, while we made out. I never thought I'd choose a dance in a high school gym over making out, but I was up to here making out, I think. I was hungry to get back to the action, and to be part of things again, to have Nicki there with me.

"Let's go!" she said suddenly. "Do you want to stay?"

"Go where?"

"Back to Kingdom By The Sea."

"Why?"

"Because everything's in full swing, Eri. I hate to stay until things are over. . . . And we're ninth in that march!"

I just looked at her. "So what?"

"Dill did that purposely. Nine is a mystical number, not lucky!"

Dill knew as much about mystical numbers as Nicki knew about slumber parties. "Dill didn't do anything," I said. "Nine was what came up. What's wrong with nine?" I said. "No, don't tell me."

"What's wrong with nine?"

"Don't tell me," I said again. "I don't want to know what's wrong with nine."

"There were nine rivers of hell," Nicki said, "and the Hydra had nine heads."

I thought of the time in Jack's Mustang when he said Help me figure this girl out! I'd given him some zinger for an answer.

"I'm serious, Eri. I'd hear my mother warn about nine. Haunted people have to throw black beans over their shoulders and say, 'Avaunt, ye spectres from this house!' nine times. Nine, our cat? He's haunted."

That was when Roman Knight's black cane tapped against the rear window, and when we heard him barking. Heard other guys laugh and bark.

I thought that would do it. That would be the final straw, and I reached down into my trousers for the keys. They were inches away from the ignition when Nicki said, "He thinks he's going to intimidate me so I'll leave? Now I won't!"

"What about nine?" I said. "What about rivers of hell and the Hydra and your haunted cat?"

"Don't make fun of me, Eri. Please?" Then she said, "Does Dill know her initials are inside the ring you're giving me?"

"No."

"I wish she knew."

"I know you do," I said. "That much I know about you."

"I want to go back to the girls' room and fix my eyes," she said. "I almost cried, but I'm all right now."

When we got out of the SAAB, we could hear Roman Knight calling out Nicki's name from behind a row of cars. "Nick-ki? Woof woof!"

"What am I going to do about him?" she said.

"Bark back?"

She surprised me by laughing, hanging on to me. "I love you because you're funny. I like funny. Jack was never funny. Even Ski was never funny. Am I funny?"

"You're funny. But not ha ha funny."

"Do you love me anyway?"

"I love you, Nicki, but you're not easy."

"You had easy," she said, "and it bored you. When we get inside that plastic ring, do we kiss?"

"First I give you the ring."

"Let's kiss first," she said. "I can't stand to be one of the bunch."

"Don't worry about it," I told her.

The march was beginning to form as she ducked into the girls' john, and I went into the boys', across from it.

Jack and I were the only ones in there.

It was the first time we'd faced each other alone since the night he'd sat in the wet paint, in our kitchen. That long.

He didn't say hello or how are you. I didn't expect him to. He mumbled something I couldn't hear, and I didn't ask him what it was. He wasn't dressed for the dance. He was in old 501s and a sweater, with a bomber jacket over it, his blond hair longer, falling into his eyes.

"Has she said she wants to leave yet?" he asked me. "She will."

I didn't say anything back. I walked up to the urinal and unzipped.

He said to my back, "I wondered if you'd show up here tonight."

"I didn't think you would," I said.

"I brought Dill. She didn't have a date."

I kept my mouth shut.

"I didn't have one, either," he said.

"Well, you don't like dances," I said.

"I like them. I just never learned to dance. I was never very fast on my feet, not like you."

"You're fast enough on the football field," I said.

"That's the only place," Jack said, "and I never did learn to come from behind. Not like you."

When I was finished, I zipped up my trousers, turned around, and said, "Jack, I never planned it. You have to believe me."

"I believe you," he said. "I know what she's like."

"It isn't her fault, either."

"She always thought you didn't like her. That bugged her."

"I *didn't* like her."

"She'd say, 'Jack, Erick doesn't like me. What am I going to do?' I'd say, 'Sure, he likes you.' "

"I didn't. At first, I didn't."

"I'd say, 'Why wouldn't he like you, Nicki? What's not to like?' "

"Honest to God, Jack, I couldn't help myself. It was something that couldn't be helped!"

"I know that, old buddy," he said softly.

"Do you? Really?"

He shook his head yes. He smiled at me the old way.

"So's this something that couldn't be helped," he said.

The next thing I knew I was on the floor.

Eighteen

WE WERE DRIVING very slowly through a wet snowfall when she said, "Eri, is there a way you can spend all night with me?"

"I doubt it," I said. "We've got company coming for Thanksgiving, and I think my nose is broken."

"See, that's why I want to be with you all night. It's the least I can do."

"What do you mean it's the least you can do?" I said. "You sound like it's a mission of mercy."

"Well? Look at you!"

"Not like something you want to do."

"Of course I want to do it! We never did it."

"I haven't even told anyone about you. I can't tell my mother I'm staying all night at Dill's. She'd never believe it."

"She thinks *that's* still going on?"

"Of course she thinks that's still going on. I didn't tell her any differently."

"Can't you call her and tell her you got into a fight,

and you don't want to face the company just yet? Can't you say you're staying with a friend?"

"Jack's the only friend I'd stay with, and I've never stayed at Jack's."

"I can see why." She laughed. "I'm sorry to laugh. Do you hurt a lot?"

"A lot," I said.

She was sitting so close, she could just reach up and touch the egg on the back of my head.

"Don't," I said. "It really does hurt. And I have to concentrate on the road. I can't see a damn thing, either. My right eye's closing."

"We're two roads away from mine," she said. "I'll watch. . . . How come you never told anyone about me?"

"You don't know my family. They'd want to meet you. If you think Jack's family gave you the once-over, you should see mine."

She lighted a Merit, blew out a stream of smoke, and said, "Don't they even wonder why you and Jack aren't friends anymore?"

"They don't know anything that's going on in my life lately."

"Daddy always knows what's going on in mine," she said, "but it's like he's been in shock since my mother died. He tries to recapture his youth with all those kids who hang out in the bar."

"They're older than you are," I said.

"No they're not. Just in years. Daddy calls them The Gnats. They're good for business, but they get on Daddy's nerves. See, he loved my mother. Really. If I ever loved anybody that hard, I'd take sleeping pills and walk into the ocean."

"Nicki," I said, "I almost got my back broken because of you. I don't even want to hear that you'd take sleeping pills and walk into the ocean if you ever loved anyone that hard."

"You know what I mean, though, Eri. I'm talking about dark, flawed passions. I'm attracted to them, but I'm also afraid of them. They drag you down."

"So does a fat lip and a cracked rib! Jesus! What are you going on about suddenly? I'm a basket case! Did this happen to me because of some little lightweight thing I got into with you?"

"No," she said.

"What the hell are you talking about then?"

"I'm just talking," she said. She quickly changed the subject. She said, "Anyway, nothing stopped that stupid march, did it? No fight could stop them from lining up with their school rings in their wet little hands."

"Who says they had wet hands?"

"Oh, they were all nervous and excited over that march, so you know they had wet hands, probably wet their pants, too. . . . I didn't say anything to you because I know you had your heart set on it, but I'd rather be in a march to the garbage dump than in that one. Jack did us a favor."

"Some favor."

Nicki had her hand, with my ring on it, on my knee.

"You know what I said to Jack?" she said. "This is your turn here, on the right, Eri."

"I see it." I made the turn, feeling the pain in my left shoulder. "What did you say to Jack? I didn't even know you spoke to him."

"I shouted at his back. 'Anybody who'd do that to his best friend is a scumbag!' . . . Roman Knight goes, 'I thought *I* was the scumbag!' "

"What about what I did to *Jack*?"

"You didn't really do anything," she said. "I had my eye on you the first day I met you. The night we went out to Dunn's? Way back then."

"You did not."

"I did, Eri. Only I thought you didn't like me, and I'd never get you away from Dill Pickle."

I sighed. "Don't make things up. You told me yourself you didn't start noticing me until we talked at Pete's apartment that morning."

"That's what I told you," she said, "but that wasn't how it really was. Why would I have planned that whole New York weekend?"

"To see Bruce Springsteen," I said.

"No. Way before then I knew. I knew that day in

the stadium when I tried out for pom-poms? You were a challenge to me because I knew you didn't like me."

"Nicki, I feel bad enough," I said. "I think my nose is broken. I might have a brain concussion. Don't tell me you had some Machiavellian scheme going to get me away from Dill way back in early September."

"What's a Machiavellian scheme?"

"Something characterized by craft and deceit," I said.

"That describes it perfectly!" She laughed while we went over the drawbridge. "How do you spell that? I want to remember that."

When we got out of the SAAB, I said, "Where'd all the cars come from?"

"You mean all six cars?" she said. "Holidays we always get a few guests. I remember Thanksgivings we'd be full up. . . . Are you going to have turkey tomorrow?"

"If they strain some for me, I might get it down," I said.

She laughed and grabbed my hand. "Anyway, it's still early. It's not even midnight, so we can go to Dream Within A Dream, and I'll make you feel better."

"Promises, promises."

"Want to bet I can?" she said, as we headed toward the entrance to Kingdom By The Sea. "We're going to have turkey tomorrow, too, if our cook is sober. Our new cook looks like Ozzy Osborne."

She was launched on some story about Ozzy Osborne checking himself into the Betty Ford Clinic to get off drugs and alcohol. She'd read an interview with Ozzy Osborne in *Circus* magazine.

When we got inside, Toledo was out from behind the front desk facing down some short fellow with glasses and black curly hair.

". . . that's when I found out Ozzy was married," Nicki was saying.

The short fellow was asking Toledo if it was customary to listen to other people's conversations at the bar.

Nicki whispered to me, "Not only customary, but it's Toledo's only recreation. He's got radar ears, Daddy says."

"Nicki?" Toledo said. "Take the desk a minute, will you?"

"Shall I take it upstairs with me?" she said. "We're going upstairs, Toledo."

"Just stand here a minute until Cap gets back. This party's checking out."

Then Toledo said, "You can wait out in your car," and the short fellow was all red in the face, staring up at Toledo, but backing away, too.

"Out in your car," Toledo said, and he got him all the way to the door.

Nicki was standing by the desk in her jacket with the traffic accident on the back, putting out a cigarette in the ashtray.

Toledo went outside with the fellow.

Nicki just said, "Shall we get some Cokes from the bar to take up with us, Eri?" as though that sort of thing went on all the time.

So I shrugged and said I'd rather have some ice, for an ice pack.

Nicki reached up and played with the little crocodile I had around my neck, looked all over my eyes, and said, "The ice would only melt? You know, Eri?" and the way she looked at me, and the way she said it, proved she could make me feel a lot better.

I could hear Billy Ocean's "Loverboy" playing in the bar. Nicki was smiling at me. I was thinking of how I'd like to spend all night up in Dream Within A Dream.

Then Toledo lumbered back inside and came over to us, wiping his mouth first with the back of his hand, then with the front, as though he was getting rid of any awful remnants left of something gross.

Toledo said, "These two guys register, go to the bar, have an argument in there about going someplace tomorrow where some guy has that AIDS disease. Four-eyes there"—pointing his thumb over his shoulder at the door—"doesn't want to go. His friend tells him to stay here, and he'll come back after dinner and get him."

Nicki was shrugging off the information when I heard the familiar Oklahoma twang, and saw Cap starting down the spiral stairs, with Marty Olivetti following him, carrying suitcases.

". . . doesn't matter if we overheard it," Cap was saying. "We're asking you to go peacefully. I don't want to fight. The bar bill's on us. Okay? We can't have anything to do with anyone visiting someplace where there's that disease."

That was the point when Marty looked down and saw me.

That was when he said, "Erick!"

"Hi, Marty!"

"I didn't think I was going to see you until tomorrow!" he said. "What the hell are you doing here?"

He pronounced it "hail."

As he got closer, he did a double take when he saw my swollen face. "Did someone beat up on *you*? Who got you involved in this thing?"

He pronounced it "thang."

I took a very deep breath and then, slowly, began letting it all out.

Nineteen

I TOOK MARTY HOME with me that night, and he stayed in Pete's old room.

Shawn drove their Buick back to Connecticut.

"I shouldn't have sprung it on Shawn at the last minute," Marty said. "I kept putting off telling him about Pete. Shawn's a hypochondriac, anyway. AIDS scares the shit out of him. I don't want Pete to know anything about this, Erick."

I told Marty I didn't want my family to know about Nicki, or my fight with Jack.

Together we concocted a story to explain how I got beat up, and how I'd connected with Marty.

I said there was a fight at the Ring Dance, caused by some drunken kids from Holy Family High, who'd crashed it. I said I'd chased them all the way out to Kingdom By The Sea in the SAAB. Then I'd found Marty, who'd come in by train and taxied out there without a reservation, only to find them all booked.

"I didn't even know that tacky place was still in business!" Mom said.

Marty said, "Well, it was its name that attracted me to it. I wrote my master's on symbolism in Poe. When I saw the place, it looked like it was right out of Poe, too!"

Then Marty went up to see Pete and Jim, in Pete's apartment, and Mom insisted on cleaning up my face with a warm, wet washcloth.

Dad was in his study, on the telephone with Dr. Kerin. Pete had reacted badly to his last round of chemotherapy.

"What happened to Dill?" Mom wanted to know.

"She's sort of mad at me, Mom."

"I can hardly blame her. Since when do you go looking for a fight?"

"It's a long story, Mom. I'll tell you someday, okay?"

"Why didn't Jack help you? Oh, I forgot. He doesn't like dances."

"Ow!" I complained. "That hurts!"

"Sorry. . . . Do you really think Shawn went to his family's?"

"Why wouldn't he?"

"I'm just oversensitive, I guess. Something about the way Marty's eyes blinked fast when he said Shawn couldn't come. When I talked to him on the phone, he said they wouldn't miss it for anything. He said

Shawn and he had just finished discussing what they'd do for Thanksgiving, and they hadn't made any plans."

"It doesn't matter, Mom."

"It matters—but I'm going to try to put all that out of my mind. Something happened tonight that's upset us all."

"I know. Grandpa Rudd said he's not coming for Christmas."

"Not that, honey. I hired two women from All Jobs to help me tomorrow. The manager called tonight to say Mrs. Tompkins had applied there, saying she quit here after twenty years because there was someone living here with AIDS. Mrs. Tompkins wanted it kept confidential, but the manager felt he couldn't send anyone out to us. . . . Pete took the call."

"I thought Mrs. Tompkins was going to Ohio to live?"

"Apparently she decided against it. . . . Poor Pete took the call."

"You said that. Well? What did Pete say?"

"He looked crushed. Then Jim arrived. We haven't had time to discuss it. . . . Your right eye looks just awful, Erick!"

"I'll be fine."

"So I suppose word is out now. It was bound to happen eventually. I'd hoped we'd have more time before it all came down on us. You should have seen Pete's face."

"I'm glad I didn't." I kept seeing the look on Nicki's face when I told Cap that yes, Marty was visiting us— it was my brother who had AIDS.

It was a strange look, almost like the expression that would come on her face when you were telling her something and she was trying to listen to a song at the same time, eyes sort of glazed over, not responding to what you were saying. I kept watching her while Cap said how sorry he was to hear about my brother, but I could understand his position, couldn't I?

I don't know what I answered. Marty said something in an angry tone, but it didn't register with me. I kept trying for eye contact with Nicki. She wouldn't look at me until I started toward the door, turned around, and said I'd call her when I got home.

"Yes," she said. She sounded dazed, distant.

After Mom finished going over my face with the wet washcloth, I went up to my room and dialed Nicki's number.

She was crying.

"Daddy doesn't want you here," she said. "He says you never should have gone in the pool with something like that in your family."

"It's not in my family," I said. "Just my brother has it."

"Why didn't you tell me, Eri?"

I couldn't think of an answer.

"Daddy says if anyone ever found out you went

swimming in City By The Sea, we'd be ruined!"

"*I* don't have it!" I said. "Nicki?"

"What?"

"*I* don't have it, for God's sake!"

"You could have it without knowing it, and give it to someone else. Daddy read that in a newspaper."

"That's not true, Nicki. I can show you that in black and white!"

"Maybe *I* could get it now."

"*I* don't have it, Nicki! Pete has it, and I can't catch it from Pete! Do you think I'd do that to you?" I asked her. "I love you. Do you think if I could give it to you I'd—"

She didn't let me finish. "You should have told me, Eri."

"I didn't tell you anything about my family. You don't like all that family-around-the-table crap. You told me that yourself."

"This isn't family-around-the-table. This is something in your family I have a right to know about, Eri. Eri? Do you know what I think?"

I didn't want to hear what she thought. I had a dread of what she'd say next.

She said, "I think you chose me so you could hide out from all of them."

"I did what?" I'd heard her.

"You chose me so you didn't have to ever talk to

Jack again, or tell Jack and Dill about your brother. They don't know, do they?"

I pressed the mouthpiece of the phone to my chin without saying anything into it. I started a cut by my mouth bleeding again, I did it so hard.

Nicki said, "None of them know, do they? That's why you chose me."

"I thought you chose me," I said. There were tears rolling down my cheeks.

"Yeah, that's what I thought," she said. "Once."

"Nicki?" I tried to keep my voice level. "I'd like to bring out a pamphlet about this thing. It explains that you can't get it from casual contact."

"Casual contact," she said sarcastically.

"*I* don't have it!"

"Does that pamphlet explain why you didn't tell someone you supposedly loved that it's in your family?"

"No," I said, "it doesn't explain that. . . . I'll try to explain that."

"I don't see how you can," she said. "I want to hang up, Eri."

I knew she was crying, too.

"Can I come out later tomorrow?" I asked her.

"Daddy doesn't want you here."

"Can we meet somewhere?"

"Not tomorrow, Eri."

Then she said, "I loved you."

Love in the past tense. Then the click, and the dial tone.

I don't remember much about that Thanksgiving dinner.

I do remember Jim Stanley hitting the side of his wine glass with his knife, at the start. "I want to propose a toast!"

He stood up. "Let's be thankful for all the good times—they were the best of times! Let's be thankful for all the good friends—they are the best of friends! I drink to sweet memories and to today! I drink to the Rudds! I drink to Pete's friends: Marty and Stan and Tina . . . and I drink to Pete! . . . Oh, and let's be thankful that Pete's kid brother isn't in top form this Thanksgiving dinner, because I've seen him eat, and *forget* second helpings for the rest of us if Erick was himself today!"

Everyone laughed and raised their glasses to clink them together.

And I remember the point when Dad spoke up. "Erick's little run-in last night reminds me of an Irish joke your friend, Shawn, would have appreciated, Marty."

Dad must have gotten his Irish jokes out of mothballs the moment he'd heard someone named Shawn was invited to dinner.

I said, "Oh, he's not going to tell a joke, Pete! Oh, it's going to hurt more than my poor bones do!" I was forcing myself to get into the spirit of things, remembering Mom's saying earlier that it could be Pete's last Thanksgiving.

"How does a newspaper story about an Irish social event begin?" Dad persisted.

"How *does* a newspaper story about an Irish social event begin?" Marty said.

"It begins, 'Among the injured were . . . '"

Dad followed that with a joke about how tough Malone's wife was (she could knit barbed wire with two crowbars!) and another about an Irish psychiatrist who used a Murphy bed instead of a couch.

I looked down at the end of the table where Pete was sitting. Our eyes met, and he rolled his to the ceiling. I wondered if he was remembering the night on the beach long ago, when we talked together about why Dad always told jokes in social situations—the same night Pete made that kite that took off in the darkness, blinking out over the ocean, its phosphorescent tail glowing under the stars.

My last memory of that Thanksgiving meal is Pete standing to make a toast at the end.

It came after the dessert course, for which Mom had opened another bottle of champagne.

Pete wasn't drinking, but he stood up with a full glass, thin and pale in his navy-blue suit, white shirt, and blue-and-white-striped tie. He held the glass up, and the light from the chandelier and the candles sparkled against the crystal.

"*Amité, doux repos de l'âme*," Pete said. "Friendship, sweet resting place of the soul . . . I love you all."

Monday morning in the hall outside homeroom, Nicki returned my ring with a note.

Now, don't try to start up something again when it's all over, Eri. Please. Let me alone. N.

It was the same morning the S.A.T. scores came in, mine lower than the earlier ones.

So I told myself I would let her alone until she couldn't stand it anymore. I wouldn't make the first move.

I stayed close to home, following bursts of studying with long daydreams of her up in my room, my mind torturing me with all the old snapshot memories of us. I played R.E.O. Speedwagon's "Can't Fight This Feeling" over and over, and thought of making love in Dream Within A Dream, High Horse on its side on the rug, Scatter watching us cross-eyed from the bureau. I saw us riding Kevin Cronin in the pool with the daffy New York skyscrapers lit up around the walls, rock music blasting in City By The Sea. I remembered her coming toward me in the halls of Seaville High in her fishnet stockings with the porkpie hat tipped over one eye, while my blood jumped, and I could hear the husky voice start a sentence, "See," . . . and I could remember helping her out of that crazy jacket with the traffic accident on the back, a moment before she turned around and put her arms up behind my shoulders. Through it all, there was the scent of First, enveloping the memories like a sweet fog moving in to wrap us in our own cocoon.

Several times I'd see her ahead of me at school, and once, impulsively, I made a move, walked fast, and heard her tell me "No!" over her shoulders. And there were all the notes I wrote and never sent, one fifteen pages long. She must have known, too, that the calls she got, when no one spoke, but only listened to her say, "Hello? Hello? Hel-*lo!*" were all from me.

Times I saw Dill and Jack, neither of them looked into my eyes.

I grew accustomed to being the loner, going home at noon for lunch, making no attempts to hang out before or after school.

In all my talks with Pete I never brought up Nicki, told him only that the thing with Dill had run its course.

"Where's Jack?" he asked me once.

"I think that's run its course too. We're not getting along."

"Is it because of me?"

"Not at all, Pete. It's school stuff."

"Does he know about me yet?"

"No." I didn't know who at school knew, or if anyone besides Nicki did. I didn't know who outside school knew either. Mom and Dad said that it was just a matter of time before all Seaville would hear the news.

"Maybe you should tell Jack," Pete suggested. "Maybe whatever's going down between you two really *does* have something to do with me. Did you ever think about that?"

"Next thing you'll say is Mom says I'm handling all this too well," I teased him.

"I just hope we're *all* strong enough for whatever comes, when it comes, Ricky," Pete said.

"Well, we're going to hang together," I said. "Family is first."

"Why the hell do all of Dad's old chestnuts suddenly sound good to me?" Pete said.

"I hope you're not going to join The Hadefield Club," I told him. "I hope you're not going to start telling corny jokes."

"Maybe this thing's affecting my brain." Pete laughed.

Then one morning at the beginning of Christmas week, I saw her look up as I was passing her in the hall. She was opening her locker, dressed in some sort of very long white coat, with white boots on, and a white scarf around her neck.

She was smoking, getting ready to drop the cigarette and step on it, something I'd seen her do so many times, and then she'd pick up the butt, with the smoke still streaming out of her nose, and she'd stick it into a Kleenex, to throw away.

I said, "No smoking, lady, you're on school property."

"Are you going to tell on me?" It was the first thing she'd said to me in weeks, and she was smiling, with one eyebrow raised.

"Maybe," I said. My heart was pounding. I kept on going, though, and she called after me, "Don't tell everything, though, Eri!" I heard the old, familiar laughter, triggering all the things I still felt, making my blood rush again the old way. I was smiling, walking off the ground, high, climbing.

It was all I needed.

I couldn't find her in the crowd after school. I figured she'd gotten out of there fast, the way she always did, and I knew where I was going, even though I was due at the bookstore. It was a Tuesday.

I thumbed a ride out to Kingdom By The Sea.

I walked across the drawbridge under a sky as blue as I'd ever seen one, with lush, white, cottony clouds and the sun inching over to change to red and set.

I didn't care if Cap saw me coming, or if Toledo did, and I wasn't surprised when no one seemed to be around as I went through the front door, because I had an idea it was the right time for this move.

I went up the spiral staircase, thrilled to be back, and down the carpeted hall I knew like I knew the back of my hand, headed straight for Dream Within A Dream. . . . *All that we see or seem Is but a dream within a dream.*

Scatter was curled up on the bed with Nine, and Nicki's closet door was open, with all her sky-high heels hanging there in bags, the crazy clothes on hangers, the hat boxes stacked on the floor. . . . I drank it all in, remembering the Sunday afternoon we'd run in there wet, shivering, new from making love, leaping under the covers. (It's so late. . . . It's gotten so dark out. . . . Have you got a phone I can use? . . . Erick, not yet . . . not yet.)

I walked across to the window and looked out.

I saw her in the distance, on the dunes.

She was all in white, and he was in black, that same long black overcoat he'd worn to the Ring Dance. I watched her take the black cane from his hand, put it up behind his shoulders, then with both hands pull him toward her.

She said something to him before she stood on tiptoe and moved her mouth up to his.

I remembered the time before we'd kissed, she'd said to me, "It's funny, because I never thought you liked me."

And I remembered how she'd said once, "See, that sleazeball doesn't like me."

When I got home, Pete asked me why I wasn't at the bookstore. He was in the kitchen, making himself an eggnog.

"I felt like being with you," I said.

I did.

"I actually finished something today, Ricky," he said.

"I just finished something, too," I said. I finally knew it, and I knew that finally I was completely on my own. "What did *you* just finish?" I asked Pete.

"Remember 'The Sweet Perfume of Good-bye'? The world where there's no fragrance whatsoever until someone starts dying?"

I nodded, wishing I could put my arms around my brother, realizing he was on his own, too, and always had been, even when he was younger than I was.

"Can I read it?" I said.

Pete said he wished I would. "I think there's still something wrong with the opening paragraph. Do you want some of this eggnog?"

"No. Thanks."

I followed him up to his apartment. He looked so little to me. I thought of all the times when I was a kid I'd walked behind him, and worried that I'd never be that big or that good.

"Why don't I read it to you?" Pete said, grabbing the manuscript from his desk and sitting down on the couch.

He said, "Remember, you were the first one I ever tried 'The Skids' out on, too? You said it gave you the creeps." Pete chuckled. "I never forgot that."

"I liked it, though. I just couldn't figure out how you'd think up something like that."

"Mom used to rearrange the furniture when she was unhappy. I'd be upstairs at my typewriter rearranging the world."

I sat across from him while he began reading.

" 'When I woke up this morning, there was a faint fragrance in my room, so subtle and exquisite, I marvel at it. And I know its meaning, but not its pain yet. That will come, for I am changing.' " Pete stopped and looked up at me. "That's not quite right. It should probably read, 'That will come, for I am bound to change.' "

"He isn't really changed yet," I agreed. "He only sees the change coming."

"Exactly," Pete said. "There's the sweetness first . . . and later on, the end."